MURDER IN THE TUSCAN HILLS

T. A. WILLIAMS

Boldwood

First published in Great Britain in 2025 by Boldwood Books Ltd.

Copyright © T. A. Williams, 2025

Cover Design by Nick Castle

Cover Images: Shutterstock

Every effort has been made to obtain the necessary permissions with reference to copyright material, both illustrative and quoted. We apologise for any omissions in this respect and will be pleased to make the appropriate acknowledgements in any future edition.

A CIP catalogue record for this book is available from the British Library.

Paperback ISBN 978-1-83518-782-1

Large Print ISBN 978-1-83518-783-8

Hardback ISBN 978-1-83518-781-4

Ebook ISBN 978-1-83518-784-5

Kindle ISBN 978-1-83518-785-2

Audio CD ISBN 978-1-83518-776-0

MP3 CD ISBN 978-1-83518-777-7

Digital audio download ISBN 978-1-83518-779-1

This book is printed on certified sustainable paper. Boldwood Books is dedicated to putting sustainability at the heart of our business. For more information please visit https://www.boldwoodbooks.com/about-us/sustainability/

Boldwood Books Ltd, 23 Bowerdean Street, London, SW6 3TN

www.boldwoodbooks.com

To Mariangela and Christina as always with love

1

TUESDAY LATE AFTERNOON

I knew it was time to stop when the figures on the screen in front of me started to blur. I glanced at my watch and saw that I'd been doing my online Forensic Cyber Security course for three straight hours now. In case I had any doubts about it, a movement at my feet told me that Oscar was also getting fed up. He pulled himself up stretched, yawned, and then looked up at me as much as to say, *Enough's enough, Dan. I need a walk.*

He was right. I knew that we both needed some fresh air so I closed the laptop, stood up and walked over to the window. It was wide open, but there wasn't a breath of wind outside, and the sticky mid-September heat that had settled over Tuscany for the past few days showed no signs of relenting. It had been a long, hot summer and it looked as though that trend was going to continue into the autumn. I looked down at my four-legged friend and saw the end of his tail wag hopefully.

'Feel like walking down to the town?'

He did.

Outside, in the shade of the cypress trees that lined the track leading to Montevolpone, it was a degree or two fresher, but I could still feel my T-shirt sticking to my back all the same. The gravel beneath my feet was as dry as a bone and the vineyards on either side looked parched. I spotted the familiar figure of one of my neighbours in among the rows of vines and went across to say hello.

'*Ciao*, Cesare, how's the harvest looking?'

It came as no surprise to see him shake his head gloomily as he bent down to study a bunch of deep blue/black grapes. 'Quality, good, but quantity a disaster. As you know, it's hardly rained at all for two months and the grapes are small. I'm sure the wine will be good, but there just won't be as much of it as there was last year.' He removed his flat cap and used the palm of his hand to wipe the sweat from his bald head. 'I've never known it so hot for September.'

I knew how he felt. Although it was a tiny bit cooler up here where we lived in the hills to the south of Florence than it was in the city itself, even here, the night-time temperature had remained stubbornly high. Thirty years working as a detective at Scotland Yard in London had taught me a lot, but not how to enjoy stifling heat. Since retiring from the force and moving to Tuscany, I could honestly say that I had very few regrets but, just occasionally, the idea of a cool summer's day in England did have considerable appeal. For the first time, I had found myself seriously considering installing air conditioning – something I had steadfastly rejected since moving in two years earlier. I glanced down at my Labrador, who was hugging the shade, and reflected that at least I didn't have a fur coat. Tuscany isn't just hot for humans.

After a chat with Cesare – who was well over seventy, but still looked as fit as a flea – I carried on down the track to the town. In spite of the heat, there was a lot of activity in the vineyards where preparations were being made for the imminent start of the *vendemmia*, the all-important grape harvest. As we walked, Oscar still managed to muster the energy to forage for pine cones and sticks for me to throw for him to retrieve. Mind you, he's only three, so fifty-four years younger than me. The idea of running about in this heat had no attraction for me whatsoever.

I pulled out my phone and called my girlfriend, Anna. She answered immediately, but in little more than a whisper.

'*Ciao*, Dan. I'm in the library. All well?' She's a lecturer in medieval and Renaissance history at Florence University and she likes nothing more than to spend hours poring over ancient manuscripts. Not really my cup of tea, but after three hours glued to a computer screen, I was a fine one to talk. Still, I thought to myself, the advantage of the library was that it had air con.

'All good, thanks. Just hot. Are you still planning on coming out here after work?' Although we'd been living together in my house out here in the hills over the summer, she had returned to her apartment in the centre of Florence for a couple of busy weeks while she prepared for the new intake of students. Her house had the saving grace of being five hundred years old. With walls twice the thickness of modern house walls, it managed to keep out the extreme heat quite successfully, but it was still more uncomfortable than out here.

'Yes, I've almost finished, so hopefully I'll be out in half an hour or so.' She then went on to show that she knows me so very well after almost a year together. 'Do you want me to pick you up from the bar in Montevolpone?'

'That would be excellent. Oscar and I are just walking down there now. See you soon.'

Twenty minutes later, I was sitting under a faded parasol, sipping a very welcome cold beer while Oscar made a right mess of the flagstones at my feet as he slurped up the bowlful of water brought by Monica, the owner. Here, shaded from the sun by the bulk of the old church, it was a bit cooler and the cold beer definitely helped. A lot.

I had been there for only a couple of minutes when my phone started ringing. It was Lina, my receptionist, PA and friend – the cornerstone of Dan Armstrong Private Investigations.

'*Ciao*, Dan. I hope I haven't interrupted your work.'

From the way she said it, I had a feeling she knew full well that I was at the bar. It was a quiet week and, although Tuesday was normally a working day for me, I had decided to stay at home to do the latest module of the highly complex cyber security course, and she knew how hard I was finding it. For somebody who had spent thirty years of his life as a Scotland Yard detective writing everything down in a little notebook, I still found computers a challenge. But in my line of business as a private investigator I didn't have any choice.

'*Ciao*, Lina. My eyes are just about starting to focus again after three hours staring at the screen. What's new?'

'I've just had a call from one of your neighbours. He says he needs your help.'

'Really? Who?'

'A man called Fausto Giardino. He says he knows you. Do you know him?'

'Fausto? Yes, indeed. His farm is only a kilometre or so from my place and he makes excellent Chianti. What's the problem?'

'He wouldn't tell me over the phone.' Lina sounded puzzled and a little bit miffed. 'He only wants to speak to you and he asks you to call him. Do you want his number?'

I copied the phone number in my notebook – old habits die hard – and thanked Lina for calling, telling her I'd be back in the office in the morning. Before phoning Fausto, I sat and thought for a minute or two. Although Oscar and I often walked past his place and I usually stopped to exchange pleasantries with him, I didn't know him as well as I had known his father, Amadeo, who had died back before Christmas. Fausto was an accountant by profession but since his father's death, he had found himself balancing two jobs: accounts and farming. Especially now at *vendemmia* time, I felt sure he must be working himself to death and I wondered whether this was what was worrying him and, if so, how I could help. I picked up the phone again, determined to give him all the assistance I could. In fairness, I did have a vested interest, considering that I had always bought my regular supply of Chianti from his vineyard and I wanted that to continue.

He answered the phone almost immediately. '*Pronto*.'

'Good afternoon, Fausto, it's Dan Armstrong. How can I help?'

'Ah, Signor Armstrong, thank you for calling so quickly.' There was a short pause. 'I have a problem.' From his tone of voice, it sounded as if it was serious.

'Call me Dan, please. What sort of problem – the sort that can be discussed over the phone or would you like to meet up? I could come to see you if you like.'

He answered instantly. 'No, absolutely not. Could I come to see you? I know where your house is.'

Although I'd been trying to keep my business commitments as far away from home as possible for Anna's sake, I was quick to agree. After all, this was a neighbour. His reluctance for me to visit him made me wonder whether maybe his might be a marital problem. I had never met his wife, although I'd seen her in the distance once. Maybe things weren't going swimmingly between them. I checked my watch and saw that it was just after six, so we arranged that he would come around at seven, but I couldn't help fishing for a bit more information first.

'Can you give me some idea what this is about?'

His voice when he replied was little more than a whisper. 'It's Maria... my wife.'

I gave him a few seconds to say more, but when nothing was forthcoming, I gave him a little prod. 'Is something wrong with her? Have you been arguing?'

'No, nothing like that. It's just that she's...' Another long pause. 'She's awfully happy.'

Of all the adjectives he could have produced, 'happy' wasn't one I'd been expecting, and I tried to dig a bit deeper. 'I'm afraid I don't see the problem, Fausto. Isn't being happy a good thing?'

'Yes... no... the thing is that she's *unusually* happy.'

Comprehension began to dawn on me. 'And you want to know what, or possibly who, might be making her so happy? Are you sure it isn't you?'

'Sorry, Dan, she's coming. I need to ring off. See you later.' And the line went dead.

I looked down at Oscar. 'Well, that's a first. It would appear that people can be too happy.'

He looked up at me and nodded towards the now empty water bowl. I felt sure that if I were to fill it with steak, he would no doubt be as happy as Fausto's wife, but somehow, I had a feeling that I was going to find that it wasn't food that was putting a smile on her face.

2

TUESDAY EVENING

Fausto Giardino arrived bang on the dot of seven and we sat down outside my house in the shade of the pergola I'd built the previous year, now festooned with roses, clematis and vines on which there were even some vestigial bunches of tiny grapes. The sun was close to the horizon and the garden was bathed in a deep ruby-red glow. As it was *aperitivo* time, Anna had insisted on preparing a tray with slices of cheese and salami while I dug out a bottle of wine. She set it down on the table, shook hands with Fausto, and then retired diplomatically into the house again. Oscar, after greeting Fausto, raised his nose, sniffed appreciatively, and cast a longing look in the direction of the salami before stretching out on the ground at my feet, one eye open just in case he might get lucky. I poured two glasses of cold, white wine and pushed one across the cast-iron table towards my guest.

'Here, Fausto, tell me what you think of this. It isn't your wine but it's one I got when I was up on the Riviera coast a month or two ago.'

He took a mouthful and swirled it around in his mouth reflectively before swallowing it and nodding. 'That's a good wine. Thank you. I like Chardonnay. Everybody seems to be planting it these days. I think maybe I need to do the same.'

We nibbled cheese and salami and chatted about grapes and wine briefly before he set down his glass and leant across the table towards me. 'Sorry I had to cut off the call before, but Maria came out of the house.'

'Still looking happy?' I did my best to keep my tone light.

'Positively beaming! The thing is, Signor Armstrong... Dan, since my father passed away, I've been working all hours and I hardly see her. During the day, I'm out in the fields and in the evenings, I have my accountancy work to do. I would have expected her to be miserable but, instead, she looks like she's won the lottery.' He caught my eye for a moment and shook his head. 'I wish she *had* won a few million, but I'm afraid it isn't that.'

I took a good look at him in the fading sunlight. He was probably still in his late thirties, although he had always tended to look a bit older. His expression this evening was definitely one of considerable concern and I hastened to add a bit of reassurance.

'Since your father's death, you and Maria have moved into your dad's house and because you're home all the time, surely she should be seeing more of you. You never know – maybe she was getting a bit lonely before, and having you around is what has cheered her up.' His expression didn't change, and I could see that he wasn't buying that so I tried again. 'Maybe she's just a naturally happy person.'

'She's always been quite a happy person but there's definitely more to it than that now.' He leant even further across the table towards me and lowered his voice. 'Earlier, while she was in the bathroom, I took a quick look in her diary. I couldn't find anything there to explain things but I did see an entry for tomorrow afternoon. It just says "3.00" and the letters "CO". Nothing more.'

'CO? Do you know anybody with those initials?'

I saw him shake his head.

'Or might it be a place? What if the C stands for café? Maybe she's meeting a friend there.'

'Maybe, but who and where?'

'I'm sure your wife must have lots of friends. Can you think of any whose names begin with O or C?'

'The only one I can think of is a woman called Claudia, but her surname doesn't start with an O and, besides which, she lives in Bologna. I can't think of anybody whose name begins with an O.'

To me, it seemed incredibly unlikely that an unfaithful wife would actually write the initials of her paramour in a diary that might be seen by her husband. The more I thought about this, the more convinced I was becoming that there had to be an innocent explanation. I took a sip of the wine and decided to approach things head-on. 'Have you spoken to her about your concerns? I can understand you don't want to let her know you've been looking in her diary but, just in general terms, have you asked her why there's always a smile on her face these days?'

'Just casually – you know, over dinner, without making a big deal of it – and every time, she gives me the same answer.'

'And that is...?'

'She's happy because she loves me.'

'Well, there's nothing wrong with that, is there?'

'No, of course not, but we've been married for four years now and I can't understand why it's taken her so long to let her love for me show so strongly. No, I think she might be happy because I'm so busy and, as a result, she's seeing less of me, which maybe means she can see somebody else more.' He caught my eye again and this time, there was almost a pleading expression on his face. 'The thing is, Dan, I love her deeply and I would hate to lose her, but somehow, I'm afraid I *am* losing her.'

I still had a feeling he was making a mountain out of a mole-hill here, but I decided to humour him. 'So what would you like me to do?'

He answered straight away. Evidently, he'd been considering this already. 'Follow her. Could you do that? I can't do it because she would recognise my car. If you could follow her tomorrow afternoon and just see where she goes and maybe even who she meets, I'd be very grateful. And if it turns out to be somebody quite harmless, then you can't imagine how relieved I'll be.'

I nodded a couple of times but felt I should be totally straight with him. 'Yes, following her shouldn't be a problem, but have you considered what might happen if I were to discover that she isn't just meeting a girlfriend, but it's something more serious – like another man, for instance? Are you ready for that? I still think you'd do much better to sit down and talk it out with her.'

I had several more tries to get him to just go home and speak to his wife but I soon realised I was on a hiding to nothing. He had clearly already made up his mind and, equally clearly, he had a stubborn streak. Finally, rather unwillingly, I agreed to follow his wife the next day and report back. We arranged that he would call me in the afternoon as soon as she left the house and I would follow her at a discreet distance. To avoid any complications, I went into the house and brought out what Anna refers to as my 'bag of tricks' – a small case filled with surveillance devices – from which I produced a tracker. I showed him how to attach this little black box, the size of a cigarette packet, magnetically to the inside of the wheel arch of his wife's car. From there, it would be invisible, but it would transmit a signal to my receiver, giving me her car's exact location.

He asked me about my charges but, seeing as he was my neighbour and also given that I had a feeling this was going to turn out to be a simple misunderstanding of some kind, I told him not to worry; tomorrow afternoon would be on me. He looked most grateful and the conversation moved on to more general matters like, inevitably, the *vendemmia* or, in his case, not only the grape harvest this month, but also the olive harvest before Christmas. He told me he had seventy-three olive trees, some over a hundred years old, and then he went on to tell me that good olive oil wasn't always easy to find and wasn't always what it appeared to be.

'You have to be so careful these days. There are so many scammers around.' He used the Italian word *imbroglioni*, which translates as cheats or scammers.

'Scammers? In what way?'

'Most people around here are still honest, but it's not the same all over. Here, we harvest the olives, take them down to the mill, and there they get pressed, producing the oil. We collect the oil, bring it back here and bottle it. We then sell it direct to locals like you, or we take it to the farmers' market.' He looked up at me and shook his head. 'But not everybody plays by the rules.' In answer to my raised eyebrows, he continued. 'Corn oil costs a whole lot less than olive oil, so what some less scrupulous people are doing is diluting good olive oil with cheap corn oil and selling it as if it was the real thing. Obviously, for people like that, their profit margins go shooting up, but the reputation of Italian olive oil goes down, and that affects all of us.'

I was fascinated. As an ex-police officer, I had come across my fair share of scammers over the years and I knew that online scams were now fleecing people left, right and centre, but I hadn't realised that crooks had moved into the olive-oil business.

'Are the police looking into it?'

He shrugged. 'They say they are, but they have enough to do as it is. After all, olive oil is only one of the scams being pulled. In my accountancy business, I keep running into victims of online fraud – some losing tens of thousands – but there are even scams involving wine and salami.'

'Salami? How can you fake a sausage?'

'It's what goes into them.' He produced a hint of a smile. 'Have you got a cat?'

I shook my head and pointed down at my snoozing Labrador. 'I don't think Oscar would approve.'

He caught my eye. 'Let's just say that in some parts of Italy, cats are in short supply.'

Comprehension – and a fair shot of disgust – began to dawn on me. 'You're saying...?'

He nodded and pointed at the two remaining slices of salami on the plate in front of us. 'That's right – miaow.' But he was quick to correct himself. 'Not this lovely *finocchiona*, of course. This is *genuino* and excellent.'

Doing my best to dismiss the unpalatable image from my mind, I returned to the subject of his wife and we arranged that I would be waiting out of sight on the lane from his farm to the main road from two-fifteen onwards the next day. He would call me as soon as his wife left home and then it would be up to me to follow her to her destination and report back. After this, we shook hands and he left, keen to return to his 'unusually happy' wife. There was still something about this that didn't sound right and I hoped my intervention would be able to rid his mind of suspicion. I went back inside and received a smile from Anna. She also smiles a lot and I've found myself smiling more and more since I met her. She raised an eyebrow.

'Solved his problems?'

'I said I'd help him out. Hopefully, I'll get to the bottom of it.' I didn't say more because I'd been trying to make a point of not discussing cases with her so as to keep my business at arm's length. My commitment to my job as a DCI in London had ultimately been responsible for my divorce, and I was desperate for history not to repeat itself.

She gave me another smile. 'I'm sure you will, *amore mio*.' We normally speak English together because her English is a whole lot better than my Italian. This is as a result of her having been married to a Brit and having spent twenty years lecturing at a university in England until her divorce and her return to Italy. She ran the back of her hand over her forehead. 'As it's so hot tonight, I'm not doing hot food. How does a mixed salad with a few slices of ham and some more of the *finocchiona* sound?'

Fausto's cat story came to mind once more but I wisely decided not to repeat what he had said. Instead, I headed to the larder and brought out the leg of cured ham on its metal stand. Since settling here in Tuscany, I had developed a distinct taste for the local ham and normally had a leg on the go at any one time. I chose the sharpest knife and set about cutting a few thin slices. The first always goes to my ever-hungry Labrador and it disappeared down his throat without touching the sides.

Over dinner, Anna told me about her day working in the library, studying the rise and fall of the all-powerful Medici family. I told her about my Herculean struggles with the cybersecurity seminar and she looked sympathetic. As we reached the end of the meal, we were sitting in the gathering dusk, unwilling to get up and turn on a light, when my phone started ringing. I picked it up and saw that it was Virgilio.

'*Ciao*, Virgilio, is this business or pleasure?'

Virgilio Pisano, formerly Inspector Pisano and now recently promoted to Commissario Pisano of the Florence murder squad, was my best friend here in Italy and the husband of my PA, Lina.

We had met a couple of years earlier and had become firm friends. I sometimes helped him out when he had cases involving English speakers, and he very kindly often passed investigative business my way that didn't fall under the police umbrella. His rank of *commissario* was roughly the equivalent of my former rank of detective chief inspector and it was no surprise that we had formed a close friendship.

'*Ciao*, Dan. It's business, I'm afraid. Might you be free tomorrow morning, by any chance?'

As far as I could remember, I had nothing pressing on my agenda this week and I always try to help Virgilio whenever I can. 'Tomorrow morning should be fine, although I've got a commitment tomorrow afternoon for an hour or so. What's happened?'

'Do you know the Podere dei Santi?'

'The luxury hotel on the way to Montespertoli? I know *of* it, although I've never had the money to go there.'

'That's the place. A body was found near there earlier this afternoon. At first sight, it appears to have been a hit-and-run accident – the poor guy was run over by a truck – but when I went out there, I got the feeling that there's something not quite right. Gianni's doing the autopsy this evening, but if he finds anything untoward, I'll need to interview everybody in the area, including all the staff and guests at the hotel and winery, in the morning. The thing is, a lot of the guests don't speak Italian, and I'd value your help with interpreting, but I'd also like to get your take on what's going on there.'

'There's a winery there?'

'Close by. I'm not sure at this stage whether it belongs to the hotel or if it's independent, but it's pretty big, and the death took place right by it.'

'What about the hotel? Who owns that?'

'An American rock star called "Digger", apparently.'

From his tone, it was clear what he thought of American rock stars. As for me, I really liked the stuff Digger and his band had produced back in the seventies, eighties and nineties and I had a number of his albums. A quick calculation told me that Digger had to be well into his seventies by now. He and the band had split up about fifteen years earlier and I hadn't heard anything much from him since. Did this mean he had now become a hotelier? Quite a career change.

'How come he owns a hotel here?'

Virgilio's tone was acid. 'They're all doing it nowadays – singers, actors, footballers, racing drivers and the like. I believe the technical term is "diversifying their portfolio". They have more money than they know what to do with, so they spread it around.'

'Well, of course, I'll be happy to help. By the way, when you say something wasn't quite right, what did you mean? Are you saying that some of the people you saw are a bit suspicious?'

'I haven't done any formal interviews, but from what I've seen, my first impression is that a few of the guests are of the "shake hands and count your fingers afterwards" variety. There looked like a little group of real hard cases there – not really what you'd expect to find in a hotel charging five or six hundred euros a night. Not all of the guests looked suspicious, obviously, but there's definitely a hard core of half a dozen. We've taken their names and we're running them through the system, and it wouldn't surprise me if we find that one or two have criminal records. I'll send you a text later this evening. If Gianni says the guy's death was just an accident, I won't take things any further, but if we turn something up, I'd appreciate your company, so, in that case, could I pick you up around nine?'

'That would be fine... No, on second thoughts I'll come in my van because I've got to get back for the afternoon and I don't want to put you out. Do you think I can bring Oscar or is the place too posh?'

'Of course you have to bring Oscar. He's part of the team now, and if they object, we'll tell them he's a sniffer dog.'

I glanced down at Oscar, stretched out at my feet, no doubt dreaming of squirrels – his sworn enemies – and slices of ham. 'When it comes to food, he's an expert sniffer. I'll wait for your text and maybe see you tomorrow. *Ciao*.'

Virgilio's text arrived at a quarter to ten that night. It was short and not very sweet.

> Definitely murder and two of the guests have
> criminal records. See you at the hotel at nine.
> Thanks.

3

WEDNESDAY MORNING

I got up early next morning and took Oscar for a good long walk before it got too hot. The sky was completely cloudless once more and I felt sorry for the farmers around here. There was no sign of Fausto Giardino as we walked past his land and I found myself hoping that my surveillance mission this afternoon would result in an innocent explanation for the smile on his wife's face. As for what awaited me this morning, I was rather looking forward to checking out the expensive luxury hotel and seeing what impression Virgilio's half a dozen hard cases had on me. Was the hotel hosting some kind of bad guys convention maybe? And, of course, there was always the possibility that Digger himself might be in residence. It would be quite an experience to meet the old rocker in person.

It took only fifteen minutes to get from my home to the Podere dei Santi – the Saints' Estate in the hills to the south. Entry was through a pair of impressive stone gateposts and up a gently curving drive flanked by iconic Tuscan cypress trees. As I climbed the hill towards the hotel, I could see a sprawling series of old red brick buildings down the slope to my right with a tractor and a pickup parked outside. It looked as though this was the winery Virgilio had mentioned.

The villa itself was magnificent. Set on the crest of the hill, surrounded by a beautifully maintained formal garden, it was a three-storey, traditional, Tuscan villa complete with dovecot in the centre of the roof. The walls were a light-ochre colour and there were dark-green, louvred shutters at the windows. Beyond the gardens were geometrically perfect rows of vines stretching out in a fan shape in all directions. The front entrance was up a short flight of stone steps with beautiful statues of Romanesque figures on plinths on either side. In front of this was a gravelled parking area, and a quick calculation told me that the combined value of the cars parked here would probably amount to almost as much as the very expensive property itself. I counted no fewer than three Ferraris, two other supercars that I didn't recognise – vehicles costing hundreds of thousands of pounds have never been my speciality – and a gleaming selection of Mercedes and BMWs. Clearly this wasn't budget accommodation.

There were four police cars parked by the entrance and I recognised Sergeant Innocenti, today in plain clothes, standing by one of them, talking into his phone. I had worked alongside him on a number of occasions and, apart from the fact that he was a conscientious police officer, I knew that he was also a nice guy. I parked alongside his car and climbed out. It was already warm in the sun but still bearable, and I went around to let Oscar out of the back of my van. He jumped out happily and made a beeline for his old friend Marco Innocenti, standing up on his hind legs to greet him. I followed him over and greeted Marco, but less effusively. As his call finished, he bent down to pet Oscar before holding out his hand towards me.

'*Ciao*, Dan. It's good to see you again.'

'*Ciao*, Marco. Tell me, does the fact that you're no longer in uniform mean something? Like promotion, for instance?'

He grinned at me. 'That's right. The boss got promotion and so did I.'

I shook his hand vigorously. 'Congratulations, *Inspector* Innocenti. So who's taken your place? Who's your right-hand man?'

He pointed into the car. 'I now have a right-hand woman – Sergeant Diana Dini.'

I glanced inside and saw a female officer deep in a telephone conversation, scribbling in a notebook on her knee. She looked businesslike and I hoped she would prove to be as efficient as the man she was replacing.

'*Ciao*, Dan, thanks for coming.' I felt a hand on my shoulder and turned to find Virgilio doing his best to fend off a boisterous greeting from Oscar with his other hand. 'Oscar, I'm pleased to see you too, but get off. Dan, things are hotting up here.' He led me across to a stone bench, conveniently situated out of earshot of anybody at the villa. He sat down and I dissuaded Oscar from climbing onto his lap as I sat down beside him. I was keen to hear the latest developments.

'You said in your message that the dead man wasn't killed in an accident. What did Gianni say?' I knew Gianni, the pathologist, pretty well by now after a few cases with which I had been involved. 'I thought you said the victim was run over by a truck?'

'That's right, but Gianni says the victim was already dead when that happened. He was actually killed an hour or so before the truck was involved.'

'And when would that have been?'

'Between two and three yesterday afternoon. The body was found just after four.'

'Do you know who he was?'

He shook his head. 'Nothing so far. His pockets had been

emptied and his fingerprints don't match anyone on our records. I've got my people checking for anybody reported missing but, again, nothing has come up so far. From the look of his hands, he wasn't a manual labourer and his only distinguishing mark is a tattoo of what looks like an eagle on his shoulder.'

'So how was he killed?'

'He was strangled with a cord or rope, tightened from behind. There are scratch marks on his neck where he must have struggled, and traces of his own skin under his fingernails.' He caught my eye for a moment. 'He was quite a small guy but, even so, whoever did this must have been big and strong – like some of the guests here.'

'You said that two of the guests have been in trouble with the law. What for?' I wagged my finger at Oscar and told him to stop pestering Virgilio. They have always been best buddies, but the *commissario* had work to do. I was impressed to see him do as he was told and wander back to sit at my feet.

'One for grievous bodily harm and the other for possession of an offensive weapon with intent.' Virgilio pulled out his notebook. 'I have yet to interview them, but I get the impression they're here as minders for three big fish.'

'What sort of big fish? Why would they need protection?'

'I have no idea as yet but I wouldn't mind betting that they're involved in something smelly.'

'How smelly? Are we talking organised crime?'

He met my eye and shrugged. 'We've sent the names to the *Antimafia* people in Rome and we're waiting for them to report back, but it wouldn't surprise me. There's just something about these guys.'

I had heard of the DIA, the Anti-Mafia Investigation Division of the Italian security services, but I had never had any dealings with them. Virgilio told me that they kept a central record of suspected mafiosi and should be able to confirm if any of the men here had links to organised crime, but I couldn't think why Mafia bosses should choose to come here to the wilds of Tuscany and I put the question to Virgilio, who shook his head in response.

'I have no idea. We're a long way from the Mafia heartlands down south but, of course, that may have been on purpose. Maybe these guys deliberately chose an out-of-the-way hotel in rural Tuscany so as not to be discovered or disturbed. Maybe they're planning a takeover or something like that, so for all I know, this could be the start of a gangland war. I've got a couple of officers interviewing the staff and I plan on interviewing the Italian speakers among the guests this morning – and that includes our suspicious characters. Language won't be a problem as long as they don't start talking to me in Sicilian or Calabrian dialect. Just to be on the safe side, I've got four officers in two cars going around all the houses in the area as well, questioning everybody they find, in case it turns out he was killed by one of the locals.'

'What's the story on the winery? I saw it as I drove in and it looks like quite a big enterprise.'

Virgilio glanced at his notebook. 'The winery and the hotel both belong to this character called "Digger". The hotel is managed by a man called Ernesto Valentini and the manager of the winery is called Fabiano Mancini. Apparently, the wine they produce is called Rockstar Chianti. If you've got it, flaunt it – although I've never heard of it before.' He sounded unimpressed. 'The manager of the hotel seems straight enough, but I'll interview him properly this morning. My people questioned the staff at the winery yesterday and told me they didn't appear to be involved in any way, but I need to go down there myself at some point.'

'So we're concentrating on the hotel for now? What about the owner? Is he here or is he still back in the US?'

'The owner is allegedly in residence. He's been here for a few days and he'll be leaving soon, presumably to visit another of his properties somewhere else in the world. I thought you and I should interview him first as a matter of protocol, but I've been told by his PA that "Digger" doesn't get up until mid-morning and normally doesn't interact with other people until midday at the earliest. If you think that's weird, wait until you see the PA. I won't spoil the fun by telling you about him in advance, but I assure you that you'll be impressed when you see him.'

This sounded intriguing. 'I'll look forward to meeting both of them. I'm quite a fan of Digger and the band so if I were doing it properly, I should have worn a bra for him to sign, but maybe he's past that kind of thing by now. So you want me to start on the English-speaking guests?'

'That's right. Apart from the dozen or so Italian speakers, there are thirty-six other guests here of eight different nationalities, and I'd be grateful if you felt like helping Marco when he interviews them. You know, the usual: what are you doing here? Where were you between two and four yesterday? Did you notice anything suspicious? I'm sure he'd appreciate it.' He grinned at me. 'This is his first murder since being promoted to inspector and having you at his side would be a great help.'

Although I felt a little twinge of regret that I wasn't going to see the suspected mafiosi for myself, I told him I'd be more than happy to help.

After that, we got up and walked back across to the police cars where Marco introduced me to his new sergeant. She was a tall woman and she looked very smart in an immaculately pressed uniform, but I couldn't help noticing that she appeared nervous.

'Sergeant Dini, this is Dan Armstrong. He's a good friend of mine and of the *commissario* and he's worked with us a number of times. Keep a close eye on him. You could learn a lot from him.'

Virgilio added a few words of explanation. 'Dan used to be a *commissario* in the Scotland Yard murder squad. He's really good at sniffing out clues.' He smiled and pointed towards Oscar, who was wagging his tail enthusiastically, having worked out that he was being introduced to a member of the opposite sex. 'And this is Oscar, and he's pretty good at sniffing as well.'

The sergeant shook hands with me and patted Oscar, but I could see that she was uneasy so I called him and he trotted good-naturedly back to my side and sat down. I gave her a smile and asked how long she'd been working with Marco and Virgilio and her reply explained her nervous appearance.

'I only started on Monday, sir.'

'No need for the "sir"; just call me Dan.' Little wonder she was looking like a cat on a hot tin roof. She had only just started, so this meant she was still very much on probation, and I knew from experience what she must be going through, trying to fit in alongside a well-established duo. I gave her an encouraging smile. 'Well, you couldn't ask for better mentors than these two gentlemen. I'm sure you'll do fine.'

She shot me a grateful look and turned to Marco. 'Shall I go and put together a rota of suspects to be interviewed, Inspector?'

Marco nodded. 'And I'll come with you.' He turned to me and glanced at his watch. 'It'll take us a bit of time to arrange the list of names and to collect everybody together. If you and Oscar want to do a bit of looking around first, could we meet back here at nine forty-five?'

I nodded in agreement. 'In that case, I think I might go down to the winery and take a quick look at where the incident happened.'

I glanced down the hillside towards the red brick farm buildings and a quick calculation told me I should easily be able to
walk down there and back in half an hour, so I bade them all
farewell and set off down the drive again. I remembered seeing a
track leading off the drive towards the farm, and Oscar and I
turned onto this and headed downhill. As we walked, Oscar
brought me sticks to throw for him to retrieve and I studied my
surroundings as we played fetch. This was archetypical Tuscany
– gently rolling hills, rows of vines and olive groves. Above us, a
pair of doves cooed in harmony, and lizards at our feet darted for
safety as our shadows fell on them. The track itself was one of
Tuscany's famous *strade bianche*, dressed with dusty white chalk
gravel. Under other circumstances, it would have been idyllic,
but no doubt the man who had been strangled and then crushed
by a truck wouldn't have agreed.

As we approached the winery buildings, we were greeted by a
volley of aggressive barking from a large, hairy mongrel with an
impressive mouthful of teeth. As a precaution, I called Oscar to
my side just in case the beast took exception to the presence of
another dog on its territory. Luckily, the barking attracted the
attention of a red-haired man who emerged from one of the
buildings. Inside, I could see large, stainless-steel tanks, presumably either containing last year's wine or being prepared for the
fresh wine coming later in the month when the *vendemmia*
started. The man was probably in his forties, thickset, and he
looked little more welcoming than his dog. He shouted a terse
command, which had the desired effect, and the big dog stopped
barking, although sinister growls continued to emanate from it. I
walked across to the man and affected a businesslike air.

'Good morning. I'm working with the police investigating the
death of a man here yesterday. Do you mind if I take a look
around with my sniffer dog?' I glanced down and saw that Oscar

had developed a fascination with a corner of an old water butt and was sniffing it assiduously but I doubted if that had anything to do with the investigation.

The man shrugged and pointed to his left.

'Help yourself. The body was found just a bit further along that way, past the main entrance, on the other side of the road. The police have taped the area off and there are officers still there – or at least the last time I looked, there were.'

'Were you around here yesterday afternoon? Did you see or hear anything suspicious?'

He shook his head. 'Like I told the other officers yesterday, I was working in the vines and I didn't see or hear anything.'

'Could I have your name, please?'

'Renzi, Guido.' His tone was indifferent and his manner unhelpful. As a result, I added a little asterisk alongside his name in my notebook. Might be worth more study.

To an accompaniment of growls from the hostile mongrel, Oscar and I headed down the track to where it joined a narrow road. The large building on my left had clearly been the subject of considerable expenditure with a series of plate-glass windows installed in the brickwork, revealing what looked like an exhibition and sales area within. A variety of old agricultural machinery had been dotted around inside, along with half a dozen ancient wooden barrels, no doubt so as to give the impression of an enterprise that had been in business for decades, if not centuries.

Above the glass doors on the corner of the building was a large sign painted in gold: '*Azienda Agricola dei Santi*', above a logo composed of the letters AAS. Below it in English was the strapline, 'It's a Rockstar of a Wine'. A Swiss-registered Mercedes was parked outside and I could see a couple talking to a salesperson inside the store. Just in case anybody could have been under any doubt, a blackboard was positioned at the roadside boasting proudly in English as well as Italian:

It's a rockstar of a wine and the best Chianti in Tuscany.

I had a feeling that there were many wineries in this region who would have debated that claim but it clearly showed that the owner of this place wasn't averse to a bit of self-promotion.

On the far side of the road, an area the size of a large room had been taped off and two scene-of-crime officers in overalls were engrossed in searching and photographing a stretch of the road and a deep, weed-filled ditch from all angles. Keeping a close eye on Oscar, I walked across and spoke to them. One of the officers turned towards me and I realised that I recognised him from a previous case. From his smile, it was clear that he recognised me and Oscar.

'*Commissario*, good morning. It's good to see you again.' He nodded towards the surgical gloves he was wearing and gave me an apologetic look. 'Sorry I can't shake hands, but you know how it is...'

'Yes, indeed. I'm working with Inspector Innocenti and I'm trying to visualise what happened. Could you talk me through it?'

He pointed towards the road. 'When the body was discovered, it was lying down here in the ditch at the side of the road, partly concealed by the undergrowth. It had clearly been run over by something heavy, and we've found ample evidence on the road attesting to the fact that it happened right here. From an analysis of the marks on the body, it's clear it was a big truck of some description. The lab's trying to analyse the tyre marks on the body to see if they can narrow it down to a certain make or model. It appears at first sight to have been hit-and-run, and the truck didn't stop.'

'And nobody saw the incident? Surely the winery shop must have been open yesterday afternoon.'

'It was open but nobody saw anything – or so they say. When the front door opens, it rings a bell to alert the staff, but there were no customers around at that time. The two staff members were allegedly both out back and they say they didn't even hear a truck go past.'

'How come the body ended up in the ditch? I would have expected to find it flattened on the road.'

He shook his head. 'Not necessarily. Sometimes these big wheels spit things out sideways. Alternatively, the person who dumped the body in the road might have waited until the truck had gone over him and then tipped the body into the ditch.'

I shook my head slowly in disbelief. 'Somebody with a strong stomach. At least the victim was already dead when all this happened.'

'Thank God. We're currently looking for any clues as to where the murder took place because the pathologist says he'd been dead for an hour or so before being run over. Although there are a number of footprints and tyre tracks here, it seems more likely that he was murdered elsewhere and brought here by somebody who staged a hit-and-run accident and then disposed of the body in the ditch. The victim had no ID on him and no wallet, but we've just found a car key lying close to where the body was found.' He held up a plastic bag containing a key and I took a close look at it. It was a VW key and it was attached to the remains of a yellow plastic tab with a few numbers just visible on it. I caught the forensic officer's eye.

'For my money, that looks like a rental car key, and yellow, if my memory serves me right, might belong to Hertz. What do you think?'

He nodded. 'Our thoughts as well. We're finding some tiny fragments of plastic scattered on the road surface, so obviously the key fob was crushed at the same time as the body. You never know, we may be able to get enough to give us the car number if it was written on there.'

'Which means that somewhere, there's a rental car without a key. Maybe up at the hotel? Have you told Inspector Innocenti or the *commissario*?'

'Not yet, we've only just found the key.'

'Let me take a photo of it and I'll tell them when I see them. I'll be going back up there again in a few minutes.' I pulled out my phone and shot off a couple of photos before taking a long, hard look up and down the road. 'So, given that the victim was already dead, the truck driver must surely have seen the body lying in the road as he came down the hill towards where we are now, or as he pulled out of the winery itself. He can't have been travelling fast on this narrow, windy road, so why didn't he stop in time? I suppose he might have been drunk or not paying attention, or maybe he was in on this as well. Certainly he can't have missed the fact that he'd driven over somebody. Commissario Pisano tells me the victim was strangled between two and three yesterday afternoon and the body was discovered shortly after that.'

'At ten past four so, like I say, the victim had been dead for over an hour before being run over. The body was discovered by the woman who lives in that little cottage. She was in serious shock yesterday, but she's looking a bit better today.'

'Does the winery have CCTV?'

He shook his head. 'Yes, but it stopped working yesterday.'

I gave him a sceptical look. 'What an unfortunate coincidence. I don't suppose it stopped working around two o'clock by any chance?'

'We had the same thought and we asked, but the manager says it happened early in the morning, and there's no way of proving it either way.'

I thanked him and left him to continue with his work while I walked across to the little cottage. As I approached the front door, I saw the lace curtain on a downstairs window twitch and the door was opened before I reached it by an elderly woman wearing an apron and holding a broom.

'Can I help you?' She glanced uncertainly at Oscar. 'Are you with the police? Is that one of those sniffer dogs?'

'Good morning. Yes, I'm working with the police.' I glanced down at Oscar, who was eyeing up a plant pot by the door, and I hoped he wouldn't let me down by comporting himself in a manner unbefitting an animal on duty – like by cocking his leg against it, for example. 'This is Oscar. We work as a team. I wonder if I could ask you about yesterday afternoon. Before you found the body of the unfortunate victim out there yesterday, did you hear any cars or trucks go past?' Since I'd been down here, I hadn't seen a single vehicle on the narrow lane. A big truck must surely have been unusual and I got the impression that this little old lady didn't miss much.

She shook her head – maybe a bit too quickly. 'I'm sorry but I didn't hear anything.' She turned her head and pulled back her grey hair, revealing a hearing aid. 'I'm afraid I don't hear so well these days. I already told the other officer that yesterday.' It sounded like a well-rehearsed speech, and I wondered if she might be hiding something.

'I see, thank you. Tell me, is it common to see big trucks on this road?'

'Not often. Sometimes, one comes here to the winery, delivering stuff, or they go on along the road to other farms.'

'What's along that way?'

'That's the way to Montespertoli, but it's not the main road.'

'Can you describe any of the trucks you've seen? Can you maybe remember any writing on the sides?'

She shook her head. 'Like I told the officer yesterday, my eyesight's not very good either. I'm very sorry, but I really can't give you any help.'

I thanked her for her time and left her. Although I would have liked to go into the winery to ask the staff in there a few questions of my own, a glance at my watch told me I had to get back. Oscar and I set off past the farm buildings towards the villa once again, to the accompaniment of a fusillade of barking from the aggressive mongrel. As we climbed back up the track, I reflected on the fact that neither of the locals I'd seen at the winery had been able to give any help. The question was whether this was because they genuinely couldn't, or because they didn't want to.

4

WEDNESDAY MORNING

When I got back to the villa, I found Sergeant Dini waiting by her squad car. She held up her clipboard with names and times and told me Marco Innocenti was waiting inside. I accompanied her up the steps and through an automatic glass door into the entrance lobby. This was a long, wide, marble-floored hall with an impressive stone staircase directly ahead. On the left-hand side was a modern glass and steel counter with two receptionists positioned behind it. These were a man and a woman, probably both in their late twenties, dressed in matching blue and white uniforms. They smiled politely but made no comment as Oscar and I followed the sergeant down a wide side corridor. Before we reached the far end, she stopped at a door marked 'Library' with two police constables standing outside it. As the officers saw the sergeant, one of them tapped on the door and I heard Marco's voice telling us to come in. I found him in a room lined with bookshelves, sitting behind a solid wooden table with a single chair positioned in front of it.

He waved me into the seat beside him and I related what the forensic officer had told me about the VW key. After seeing my photos, he immediately called the constables in from outside and ordered one of them to report this information to Virgilio and then to check on all of the vehicles parked outside the hotel in case one might prove to be the missing rental car. If there was no sign of a matching vehicle here, then he should ensure that all units be instructed to keep their eyes out for a VW rental car parked or abandoned within a ten-kilometre radius.

After the constables had left, Marco repeated what his boss had already told me. 'We have no reason to suspect any of these guests in particular, so we're asking them all the same questions about yesterday: where they were, if they saw anything and so on. You know that my English is non-existent, so I'm counting on you to translate as I ask the questions and they answer. That way Dini and I can keep a record of the names and their answers. Okay?'

I nodded. 'Where are the guests now?'

'They've all been asked to assemble in the lounge at the end of the corridor. From there, we'll bring them here and interview them one by one. Shall we make a start?'

He instructed the sergeant to ask for the first interviewee to be shown in. Dini opened the door, spoke briefly to the remaining constable, and then took up position at one end of the table, her clipboard in front of her, pen in hand.

The interviews started and it very quickly became clear that the majority of the guests were here on holiday and claimed to know nothing of the murdered man. Some hadn't even been here yesterday afternoon, but had been out touring Tuscany. As we worked our way through the list of Germans, Brits, French, and an assortment of other nationalities, I took notes of my own, but put an asterisk alongside only a couple of them.

One of these was a rather flashy-looking Englishman wearing a pale-pink designer polo shirt and the sort of expensive gold watch on his wrist that street thieves love. He told us that his name was Matthew White and he came from London, where he claimed to own a chain of restaurants. His accent was more East End than Chelsea and he was probably around my age or a bit younger, maybe in his early to mid-fifties.

He was one of those people that automatically get my back up – and that wasn't just because he was a whole lot better-looking than me with his immaculately styled, suspiciously dark hair without a hint of grey. His attitude to being questioned was one of supercilious indifference and I even wondered if he had been interviewed by the police before, because he showed none of the concern or discomfort normally displayed by people when being questioned, particularly in a murder inquiry. He told us that he was here on holiday with his girlfriend for a few days and that they had been down at the pool all the previous afternoon. After he'd left the room with a dismissive wave of the hand, I turned to the two police officers.

'I don't know about you two, but there was something about him I didn't like. Considering that somebody has just been murdered, he looked and sounded as if he couldn't care less, so he's either a totally callous human being or he's an accomplished actor trying to hide his involvement. What did you two think?'

Marco glanced across at his new sergeant and put her on the spot. 'Well, Dini, what did you think of Mr White?'

She put down her pen and ran a nervous hand across the side of her face before answering. 'I agree with *Commiss*... with Dan. There was definitely something slippery about him.'

Marco nodded in agreement and I saw an expression of relief cross the sergeant's face. 'My feelings entirely. Let's see what his girlfriend has to say for herself.' He consulted his list of names. 'Signora Thompson.'

And that was when it suddenly got weird.

The door opened and the next interviewee was ushered in. I

looked up and stared in stunned amazement as I found myself face to face with none other than my ex-wife.

I swear my jaw physically dropped when I saw her, and when her eyes landed on me, she stopped dead, midway across the floor towards the table. I glanced sideways and caught the sergeant's eye, seeing a puzzled expression on her face. I knew I had to say something quickly and I started with my ex-wife.

'Hello, Helen, I wasn't expecting to see you. Do sit down, please.' As she came forward as if in a dream and took a seat in front of Marco and me, I turned to him and the sergeant and gave them a few words of explanation in Italian. 'This is Helen, my ex-wife. I had no idea she was even in Italy. She's reverted to using her maiden name.' Returning my attention to Helen, I repeated myself in English for her benefit. 'This comes as quite a surprise. I didn't even know you were in Italy.'

She had to clear her throat before speaking. 'It was a last-minute thing.' A movement at my feet told me that Oscar had sensed that here was a lady in distress – or at least struggling – and he got to his feet and trotted around to sit beside her, his nose resting on her thigh. She even managed to summon a little smile as she bent down to stroke his head.

I hastened to explain to her what I was doing here. 'As a lot of the guests at the hotel don't speak Italian, I'm here helping out with interpreting. This is Inspector Innocenti, who has a few questions for you. We're interviewing everybody.'

Seeing her again two years after the divorce had come as a shock to the system. As Marco started out on the usual questions, I studied her as unobtrusively as possible. She was looking good, very good. She was wearing a flowery dress that complemented her tanned arms and shoulders, and her hair was now a whole lot blonder than it used to be. The only thing that didn't look so good was the expression on her face. Whether this was just the shock of seeing me again or at being involved in a murder inquiry, or for some other reason, was hard to tell, but she was looking nervous, maybe even scared.

The questions were quickly over and it came as no surprise to find that she had been unable to tell us anything. She confirmed what her boyfriend had said about having spent the previous afternoon at the pool and, when asked by the inspector, she also confirmed that neither of them had left the pool until well after four, thus providing convenient alibis for each other – not that I would have suspected her of carrying out such a gruesome murder. Her boyfriend, maybe, but definitely not Helen.

The questions finished, Marco glanced across at me, no doubt offering me the opportunity to say something to the woman with whom I had shared thirty years of my life, but I found myself completely lost for words. In the end, it was Oscar who inadvertently came to the rescue. Helen pointed down at him and gave me a hint of a smile.

'And this must be the famous Oscar. Tricia's told me about him. He's a good-looking chap.'

'He's my best buddy. We go everywhere together.'

'I can see that.' She rose to her feet. 'Well, it was nice to see you, Dan.'

Uncertain what to do, I stood up awkwardly and we shook hands like two strangers, before she turned and left the room – and I slumped back into my chair feeling like a clueless teenager. There was silence for a few moments during which Oscar, realising that I was now the one who needed support, came back around the desk and sat down close to me, leaning heavily against my leg and looking up with a concerned expression on his face. I ruffled his ears while on the other side of me, Inspector Innocenti did his best to offer a few comforting words.

'I imagine that must have come as quite a shock, Dan. I've no idea how I would have reacted if one of my exes had walked in. Not that I've ever been married, of course.' He shot a quick look sideways at the sergeant, who was studiously concentrating on her clipboard. 'I thought Dan handled that pretty well, don't you, Dini?'

The sergeant flushed but she collected herself. 'Definitely, but what an amazing coincidence.' She gave me a little smile. 'At least that's one suspect we can take off the list. I can't imagine you would ever have married a murderer.'

I managed to smile back at her. 'If I had done, I'd be dead now. Things got pretty grim towards the end of our marriage.' Taking a deep breath, I did my best to put on a more professional appearance. 'Anyway, the divorce was two years ago and a lot of water has flowed under the bridge since then. Shall we carry on with the interviews? I'm ready if you are.'

It was approaching midday by the time we'd finished seeing everybody, and my list of potentially dodgy interviewees had extended to only three, and none of them looked particularly likely to have been our perpetrator. These were a nervous-looking Swede, a tall American, and my ex-wife's partner, Matthew White. I was secretly rather pleased that my suspicions of him had surfaced before I'd found out that he was now with Helen, so she couldn't accuse me of unfair bias – not that I was likely to see her again.

I talked it over with Marco and the sergeant and was pleased to find that they shared my opinion of these three. The constable outside our door relayed the information that Virgilio was still engaged with his interviews but nearing the end so I took the opportunity to slip out for a five-minute walk with Oscar. As I did so, I spotted a number of the guests wandering around now that they were no longer penned into the lounge, but I didn't see Helen and I couldn't help a feeling of disappointment.

No sooner did I recognise the feeling than I immediately started questioning what was going on inside my head. Helen had divorced *me*. She was here with another man and, more to the point, I was now happily paired with a wonderful partner of my own. Why, then, the feeling of disappointment? Did this mean something? Could it possibly be that this fleeting meeting with Helen was going to stir up feelings in me? I had loved her very dearly and had even given up the job I'd also loved in the hope of changing her mind, but she had turned her back on me and filed for divorce. Since then, I had thought – at least I had done up till now – that I'd managed to put that chapter of my life behind me, but maybe such was not the case after all.

5

WEDNESDAY LUNCHTIME

It was now blisteringly hot again and Oscar and I hugged the shade as we went for our walk. I did my best to banish thoughts of Helen by concentrating on the case. Of course, it all depended on what results Virgilio had managed to get out of his interviews, but so far, it wasn't looking very hopeful. Until such time as we had an identity for the victim, it would be near impossible to establish any kind of motive, and of the people I had seen this morning, none had leapt out at me as potential murderers – although the man with the barking dog at the winery and the little old lady had been far from forthcoming.

I kept a close eye on the front door as Oscar and I walked about in the vines until I spotted the familiar figure of Virgilio. He had just emerged onto the steps so I hurried back to him and asked the all-important question.

'Any joy with your interviewees?'

He shrugged his shoulders. 'My officers who interviewed the staff found nothing untoward so it's unlikely any of them were involved. As far as the Italian-speaking guests I saw are concerned, some were elsewhere, some at the pool, and several were in their rooms, quite possibly enjoying a bit of marital, or more probably extra-marital, bliss. The three suspicious characters and their bulky companions I spotted yesterday were in the dining room until two – and the waiters confirm their story – after which the three big fish claim to have been in a meeting in one of their suites. The bar manager told us that his people supplied them with drinks in the course of the afternoon but he can't vouch for them all being there all the time. The three minders say they were in one of the rooms next door playing cards and they never went out until five.'

I caught his eye. 'So none of them with a credible, independent alibi.'

'Indeed. As far as my gut feeling is concerned, any one of the minders could well have been capable of committing a brutal murder and the three bosses looked pretty tough as well. Definitely a very questionable bunch.'

'What about CCTV? The forensics people told me the winery CCTV wasn't working. What about here at the hotel?'

'Yes, the manager told me there are cameras in the lobby, restaurant, and lounge as well as outside in the car park. They're handing over the footage to my people this afternoon – apparently, the person who knows how to work it won't be back until three.' He held up his hands in frustration. 'Her child has been sent home from school with an upset stomach and she has to take him to his grandmother.' He looked over at me and changed the subject. 'I gather you had an uncomfortable encounter yourself.'

I nodded. 'Seeing my ex-wife was the last thing I was expecting.'

'Are you going to see her again?'

This time, I shook my head decisively. 'No, that's that. I now need to forget that I've seen her and remember that I have Anna back home waiting for me. Anyway, returning to the group of six hard cases you saw this morning, what reason did they give for being here?'

'The three bosses say they're here on business. They told me they're interested in investing in a property here in Tuscany. They referred to the other three men as their "associates", but for my money, they're not so much bag carriers as bodyguards. And this begs the question of why harmless businessmen need protection.'

'Still no word from the *Antimafia* people?'

'All I've been told so far is that they're checking and they'll email me details later today. You know what it's like in Rome: never do something today that you can put off until tomorrow.' I thought that was maybe a bit of a sweeping statement, but I made no comment. After all, I knew that Virgilio spent quite a lot of his time dealing with the ministry in Rome so he presumably knew their ways well by now.

'Why do this lot want to buy a property in Tuscany?'

'To transform it into a luxury hotel like this one, because they say this is the most sought-after region in Italy for upmarket tourism.'

'They could well be right. Where do they come from? Are they local?'

'No. One's from Milan, one from Bari and the other one from somewhere south of Naples.'

'What about as far south as Sicily?' Because we all knew which criminal organisation was based there.

Virgilio shook his head. 'Not according to their ID cards, but we'll check their backgrounds.' He knew me well by now and could see that I'd been expecting a different answer. 'But that doesn't mean we're not talking organised crime, Dan. Don't forget, the Sicilian Mafia are only the tip of the iceberg these days when it comes to the *malavita*. Let's see what information comes up from Rome.'

'Any progress in establishing the victim's identity?'

'Yes, at least we're getting there with that. One of our cars spotted a silver Volkswagen Polo parked just off the road, partly hidden in a clump of trees, only about a kilometre from here. Forensics have gone over now with the key that was found at the crime scene and we should hear pretty soon if it fits. If so, then a quick call to the car rental company with the registration number and we'll have the guy's identity.'

'Hidden in the trees, eh? If the car really does turn out to belong to the victim, then I would say there's quite a strong possibility that he left it there so he could sneak up here to spy on – or even try to murder – somebody at the hotel. What do you think?'

'I agree. There's nothing else of interest in the area apart from the winery and a few farms, which makes it more likely that he was killed by somebody here at the hotel. They then dumped his body on the road down there when a truck was coming past, in an attempt to make it look like an accident.'

'But unless it was a very dozy truck driver, he must surely have seen the body in the road and I can't believe he wouldn't have been able to stop or take avoiding action. I wouldn't be surprised if the truck driver was in on it.'

Virgilio nodded slowly. 'You may well be right, but of course the driver might have been drunk and just kept going rather than stop to report it. I've known it happen before. He would have known he would have found himself in court or in jail and almost certainly would have lost his job.'

I nodded in agreement. 'Could well be. Anyway, what we've got to do now is to work out why the victim came here to the villa. Did he come to spy, or was his motive something more sinister like robbery or even murder? I suppose he might have been a glorified paparazzo spying on our resident rock star, but I'd be surprised. After all, Digger and his band disappeared from the scene years ago.'

'Well, that can be one of the questions for Mr Digger – or whatever his real name is. His PA will be coming any minute now to accompany us to the great man.'

'Eugene Froot, that's Digger's real name.' I felt quite proud of myself. 'Amazing the bits of useless information one picks up. You can see why he changed it. It just doesn't sound right for a heavy-metal rocker, does it?'

Virgilio nodded towards the villa. 'Here's his PA now. Brace yourself.'

I followed the direction of Virgilio's eyes and saw a figure emerge through the glass doors. As he came out into the sunlight, I noticed that even Oscar pricked up his ears and stared. Digger's PA sported a long ponytail of white hair, gold earrings, a tie-dyed T-shirt in shades of orange, yellow and pink, and he was wearing three-quarter-length white shorts accompanied by open-toed sandals finished off with black socks. He looked like Yoda from *Star Wars* on his way home from Woodstock.

Spotting Virgilio, he beckoned. 'If you would like to follow me, sir, Digger will see you now.' Unexpectedly, his accent and choice of phraseology were pure *Downton Abbey*. Given his wardrobe choices, I had been expecting him to sound more weird and wacky.

Virgilio, Oscar and I followed him to the lift. He pulled out a key and inserted it into a slot in the control panel, the doors closed behind us and the lift whisked us up to a floor at the top of the building evidently off limits to normal guests. In spite of my advancing years, I felt a little shiver of anticipation at the thought of meeting one of the heroes of my youth. The PA beckoned to us to follow him down a short corridor that opened into an enormous lounge with arched windows looking out over the vineyards to the hills beyond. As a place to live, it was amazing and I could hardly believe that its owner came here only for a week or so every now and then. But, of course, I hadn't seen any of his other residences, which were maybe even more awe-inspiring.

'These two gentlemen are detectives from the local police, sir.'

At first, I couldn't see at whom the words were aimed but then a movement caught my eye. What I had assumed to be a pile of cushions dumped on a long, leather sofa turned out to be none other than Digger himself. As he heaved himself to his feet, it was hard to believe that this shrunken old man had once been capable of driving an audience of fifty thousand into a frenzy. He walked across to us, leaning heavily on a fancy, gold-topped cane, stopped to pat Oscar and then held out his free hand. His hair was streaked with grey and the lines on his face looked like corrugated iron, but his eyes still sparkled.

'Good afternoon, gentlemen. Thank you for coming. This is a terrible business.' He glanced at the PA as he stroked Oscar's ears. 'Stokes, have you offered these gentlemen something to drink?'

'I was about to, sir.' The PA turned towards us and asked deferentially, 'Something to drink, gentlemen?'

Before we could answer, another voice cut in from the door. 'Open a bottle of Bollinger, Stokey; everybody likes that.'

I turned to see a stunningly beautiful woman standing by the door wearing short shorts and a Rolling Stones T-shirt that was probably older than she was. She had long, blonde hair, even longer legs, and her face could have come from the front cover of a fashion magazine. I was trying to work out the age difference between her and Digger when he introduced us.

'My daughter, Florida. Florrie, these gentlemen are from the police, investigating the death at the winery. Yes, Stokes, open a bottle of champagne. If they won't drink it, I'm sure Florrie will.'

Oscar trotted across to greet the new arrival, tail wagging enthusiastically. I'm sure he could be used to judge beauty pageants – if such things still exist – because he definitely knows beauty when he sees it. Florida gave him a big smile, dropped to her knees, and made a terrific fuss of him.

We sat down opposite the sofa and Virgilio started by introducing us both. Although his English is pretty good, he spoke in Italian and I translated. 'My name is Commissario Virgilio Pisano of the Florence murder squad and this is my good friend and former Detective Chief Inspector at Scotland Yard, Dan Armstrong. Dan's here to help with interpreting, as my English isn't so good. We'll try not to take up too much of your time but, as you know, we're investigating the unfortunate death that occurred yesterday afternoon close to your winery.'

The old rocker shook his head ruefully. 'I'm sure your English is better than my Italian. I'm afraid my Italian doesn't go much further than "*Buongiorno*" and "*Buonasera*". Any help we can give, we will. Florrie, come over here and see if you can help as well.'

It came as no surprise to see Oscar follow her to the sofa. I readied myself to tell him not to climb up when he surprised me by sitting down primly at Florida's feet and resting his head on her knee. She stroked his ears as Stokes filled four glasses with champagne and set them on the low table in front of us. Virgilio and I made a start.

'Could I ask how long you've been here?'

'Here in Tuscany, only since Monday. We flew here from Paris, France, where Florida's been studying haute couture.' From the way he pronounced it, it was clear his French was no more fluent than his Italian. 'I'm flying back to the US next week and Florrie's staying on here with Johnny for a few days.' A flicker of antipathy crossed his face for a second and I thought it worth checking.

'Johnny?'

Florida answered. 'His name's Giovanni Riccio, but he calls himself Johnny. He and I've been seeing each other on and off.'

'And where is he now?'

'He's gone to a wine auction. He goes around buying wine most days. He'll be back later.'

'Is the wine for his own consumption or is he a dealer?'

'He's a dealer, mainly exporting to the UK and US. He buys wines all over the place, including Dad's Rockstar Chianti from our own winery, of course.'

'And now you and he are together?'

'More or less.' She didn't sound totally convinced. 'He's been coming here for several years now, but I only met him for the first time last summer. I ran into him in the vines and things have developed from then.'

From the expression on her father's face, I could see that he was far from happy about this development and I wondered if this was because he believed Johnny Riccio to be a gold-digger. I made a mental note to check the man out. Maybe he had a hidden agenda – although whether this might extend to murder remained to be seen. I saw Virgilio register this information before changing the subject.

'Please could you both tell us where you were between two and five yesterday afternoon? We're asking everybody.'

Florida answered for both of them. 'Dad and I were at the Uffizi. We had an early lunch and headed off to Florence at around one-fifteen, as we'd booked our visit for two o'clock.'

I was interested to hear that even famous rock stars had to book a slot when visiting the world-famous art gallery. 'And what about Johnny Riccio? Did he go to the Uffizi with you?'

Digger answered with a wry laugh. 'Johnny go to an art gallery? You must be joking. He wouldn't know a Botticelli if it jumped off the wall and bit him.'

'Have you any idea where he was that afternoon?'

Florida shook her head. 'You'd better ask him. He told me he had some work to do and I left him sitting out on the terrace. He was here when we got back so I imagine he didn't go anywhere.'

Virgilio and I filed that away for future reference and Virgilio continued with the questions. 'Thank you. Have either of you been down to the winery since you got here?'

Digger answered. 'Yes, on Monday afternoon. I was interested to know how this year's grape harvest was looking.'

'And how is it looking?'

'Low on quantity because it's been so hot and dry, but Mancini says it should be excellent quality.'

'That would be Fabiano Mancini, the winery manager. Have you spoken to him since the death?' Digger shook his head and Virgilio turned the question to his daughter. 'What about you, Signora Froot? Have you been down to the winery? Or your boyfriend, Signor Riccio, has he?'

'"Signora Froot" makes me feel so old. Please call me Florida. I haven't visited the winery for a couple of years now – mainly because I can't stand that Mancini man – but, now that I think of it, Johnny did say he wanted to go down there. Like I say, he buys Dad's Rockstar wine and exports it.'

I made a note of this information that might prove interesting, potentially putting Johnny Riccio and the murder victim in the same place at roughly the same time. I also noted that the winery manager hadn't been Florida's favourite person. 'What about your butler, Stokes? Did he accompany you to the Uffizi?'

Digger answered with a grin. 'Stokes would be delighted to know that you referred to him as the butler. I call him my PA, but he does a bit of everything. He sees himself as a true-blue English manservant, even though he was born in Phoenix, Arizona, and he's only visited England a handful of times. He's watched a load of old movies, though. As for the Uffizi, no, he didn't come in with us. He dropped us near the gallery and then drove back here again.'

So this meant that Stokes, too, had no alibi and, more importantly, he would have been absent for well over an hour during which time Johnny Riccio could well have taken a trip to the winery. Virgilio returned to his questions.

'Is there anybody here on the staff or among the guests who strikes you as suspicious?'

They both shook their heads and Digger answered. 'Just about the only staff we see – apart from Stokes, but he travels everywhere with me – are the maids who look after us up here. As for the guests, I know the hotel is three quarters full, which is good, but I haven't spoken to even one of them. I don't advertise the fact that I'm here.'

Florida added, 'Dad likes his privacy so he tends to avoid interaction with the public these days.'

It occurred to me that, looking as old and haggard as he did now, he could probably go almost anywhere without being recognised. I felt sorry for him but then immediately took another look at the luxurious surroundings. He wasn't doing too badly.

Virgilio carried on. 'Do you think the victim might have come here to spy on *you*, Signor Digger?'

The old rock star smiled. 'Twenty years ago, maybe, but not now. When I gave my last concert, most of today's music-loving public weren't even born. No, my days of punching paparazzi are over.' I smiled back at him. I could still remember the story of the time when he'd taken exception to a photographer sticking a camera through his bathroom window and had lashed out.

We then chatted about all manner of things from Italian art – which appeared to be of interest to both of them – to Italian food for another five minutes before Virgilio and I finished our excellent champagne and stood up. Before we left, I couldn't help telling Digger how much I liked his music and he looked genuinely pleased at the compliment. Virgilio gave Florida his card and asked her to get her boyfriend to call when he returned from his wine-buying jaunt and then we left, accompanied to the ground floor in the lift by Stokes.

Once the PA had departed in the lift, Virgilio glanced at his watch. 'It's gone twelve-thirty. I think we deserve some lunch.' He stopped and flicked his eyes across the lobby to where a group of men were standing. His voice dropped to a whisper. 'Over there are the three big fish and their minders. Have you ever seen such a suspicious-looking bunch?'

I did my best to look casual as I glanced across the lobby. Fortunately, the six men were involved in what looked like an earnest conversation. The three big fish were immediately recognisable from their clothes, styled hair and their imperious attitudes towards the bodyguards – if that was what they were. The sheer weight of gold chains and medallions around the bosses' necks, the watches on their wrists and the rings on their fingers announced that they were men of substance – or at least that they were trying to give that impression. The bodyguards varied from one the size and shape of one of the standing stones at Stonehenge to a younger man whose stomach muscles pressing against his T-shirt looked like an old-fashioned washboard. Tough guys, without a doubt.

I felt Virgilio touch my arm and saw that Marco Innocenti and Sergeant Dini had just appeared. 'As I was saying, how about lunch?' As he posed the question, I saw Oscar's ears, eyes and nose turn in his direction. When it comes to food, Oscar is a polyglot. 'However, I don't think even a *commissario* can afford the prices here at the Podere dei Santi. There's a nice little restaurant only about five kilometres from here. Who's feeling hungry?' He grinned at me. 'And Dan and I've already had a little *aperitivo*.'

6

WEDNESDAY LUNCHTIME

I gave Virgilio, Marco and Sergeant Dini a lift in my van. In the mirror, I could see Oscar breathing down the sergeant's neck over the top of the back seat, but she didn't complain. The restaurant was a new one for me even though it was only twenty minutes or less from my home. I hadn't even realised that it existed before, but that might have been because it was tucked away several hundred metres up a *strada bianca* with only a faded wooden sign at the roadside indicating that this was indeed a restaurant. The place was called *l'Istrice*, which I now knew to be the Italian for porcupine. I knew this because I'd been amazed to see one of these rare animals for myself as it had scurried across the track close to my home some months previously. I hadn't seen one since but I'd occasionally come across porcupine quills lying on the ground and now had a collection of half a dozen.

The building itself had probably started life as a barn because we walked into a high-ceilinged room with hefty wooden beams supporting the roof above. The restaurateur escorted us through the dining room and out onto a terrace on the shaded side of the building where a hint of a breeze kept us at an agreeable temperature. She then returned with a bowl of water for Oscar and a verbal menu for us. Her Tuscan accent was strong, but I managed to follow pretty well and we all chose the same thing: mixed antipasti followed by *pappardelle al cinghiale*. Wild boar season was well and truly open and the owner told us her husband had shot the unfortunate beast that ended up in our pasta sauce only a matter of metres from the restaurant.

She asked what we would like to drink and, out of interest, I suggested we try a bottle of Digger's Rockstar Chianti. The restaurateur nodded, but I saw a grimace cross her face for a second. Was this because she didn't approve of foreigners making Tuscan wine or because it wasn't very good? She went off to place the order and then returned with a bottle of 'the best Chianti in Tuscany,' a bottle of mineral water, and a basket containing bread rolls and packets of breadsticks. Oscar's acute Labrador food sense immediately told him that there were grissini available and a heavy – and hungry – head landed on my thigh as he subjected me to the full 'I'm starving' treatment. I handed him down a couple of breadsticks and watched as the owner opened the bottle and filled our glasses. Virgilio waited until she'd departed before raising his glass.

'Right, let's give this stuff a try.' He took a mouthful and swilled it around in his mouth before swallowing and grimacing. 'God Almighty, that's rough!' We all followed suit and then looked at each other. Marco was the first to comment.

'Definitely not great. Bottom shelf of the supermarket wine.'

We all nodded in agreement as Virgilio picked up the bottle and studied the label. 'Rockstar Chianti' was written in gold letters on a background of an auditorium packed with cheering faces. 'If I bought a bottle of this in the supermarket for five euros, I'd be reasonably happy, but this stuff sells for a lot more than that. After all, Chianti produced here is inside the protected Chianti DOCG area so it commands a premium.'

I swallowed my mouthful and had to agree with him. 'My local Chianti's a whole lot better than this.' Thought of Fausto's wine made me think of him and his wife, and I hoped my investigations this afternoon wouldn't uncover any uncomfortable truths and – equally important from my point of view – anything that would prevent them from continuing to make my favourite wine.

Virgilio gave the other two a brief summary of our conversation with Digger before looking across at me. 'I think we can safely eliminate him and his daughter from our inquiries, don't you, Dan?'

'Definitely. If there's any doubt in the matter, we can always check their story of going to the Uffizi. That place is absolutely bristling with CCTV, so it should be easy to confirm. As I see it, there's a question mark hanging over the head of Florida's boyfriend, Johnny Riccio, and possibly his PA. Neither appears to have an alibi for Tuesday afternoon and the boyfriend had indicated that he planned on visiting the winery. You're going to be seeing him this afternoon, aren't you? It might be worth doing a bit of digging to find out who he is, how they met and whether he's got any enemies.'

'I most certainly will, and I'll question the PA as well.' He turned to Marco. 'How did your interviews with the English speakers go?'

Marco gave him a quick summary and then we listened in as Virgilio told us more about the people he had questioned this morning.

'Let's assume for a moment that the three bosses were telling the truth when they said they were here looking for a property. Coming to a hotel like this would have been a tax-deductible jolly for them, and I would have expected there to be a few wives or girlfriends brought along but, no, just the men and their minders.'

I took a very welcome mouthful of cold water before throwing in a query. 'Do you believe their story that they're looking for a villa to turn into a hotel? Might that just be a cover for something more sinister?'

'Could be, but, until I hear more from Rome about them, it's just conjecture. Put it this way, the three big fish could be on the level, but why come accompanied by gorillas if they're clean?'

At that moment, his phone bleeped to indicate that he had received a message and he opened it eagerly. It was actually an email and he was just starting to give us the highlights when our antipasti arrived. This consisted of a selection of salami along with mixed bruschetta made with slices of the wonderful Tuscan unsalted bread. Some were topped with chopped tomatoes and olive oil, some with chicken liver pâté and some with lovely soft fresh goat's cheese and slices of pear. It all tasted as good as it looked and, understandably, it took a minute or two before Virgilio was able to pass on what he had just read.

'Well, according to the *Antimafia* people, it doesn't sound as though this is some sort of gathering of the Mafia clans. None of the three prime movers are known to have links with organised crime although, like I told you, two of their minders have a history of violence. My people have been doing a bit of digging and although none of the so-called businessmen have criminal records, they aren't saints by any means. Two of them have skeletons in their closets. A couple of years ago, Naples police suspected Luigi Bellomo of running an illegal gambling den, but nothing was ever proved, while Achille Calabrese has a video company in Milan, making porn movies and maybe not paying his taxes, but, again, nothing ever proved. It sounds as though they're maybe a bit shady, but not exactly criminal masterminds.'

Marco Innocenti voiced what I was thinking. 'So if they are on the level or maybe just a bit murky, why the bodyguards?'

I was pleased to hear Sergeant Dini prepared to get involved in the conversation as well. 'Of course, the fact that none of the three has a criminal record might just be because they're too smart. Think of Al Capone, for example. Everybody knew what he was doing but if it hadn't been for his tax avoidance, he might well have remained a free man.'

Virgilio nodded in agreement. 'So you're saying that these guys might in fact be criminals, but they just happen to be very clever at avoiding getting caught. That would of course explain the bodyguards and maybe even explain their readiness to murder somebody who was spying on them. The problem we have is proving it.'

'I suppose it's possible that the individual bodyguards are there to each protect their employer from the other two – no honour among thieves and all that – but let's assume for a moment that they *are* on the level. If they're buying a property together, does this mean they've set up a separate company or a partnership or what?' I was thinking out loud. 'And what about funds? Have they got the money to do what they say?'

'We're in the process of checking them out but, according to Davide Cassano, who comes across as the leader of the consortium, they have seven million euros reserved for this project. Like I say, we're checking, but the banks work even slower than our *Antimafia* friends in Rome do.'

The pasta course was excellent. Since I'd settled here in Tuscany, the broad strips of pappardelle had become my favourite of all the many shapes and sizes of pasta. The rich, gamey sauce was immensely tasty and it was an excellent meal –

apart from the wine. As we ate, we chatted, partly about the case but also about more general matters, and I learned that Sergeant Diana Dini was originally from Prato to the west of Florence, and her hobbies included marathon running and chess. As far as I was concerned, she could keep the marathons – I used to run quite a bit, but nowadays, walking with Oscar strikes me as a whole lot more enjoyable – but a calculating chess brain boded well for her career as a detective.

The coffees had just arrived when a call came through to Marco. He beamed as he got the news and he was quick to pass it on to the rest of us. 'The key fits and the documentation inside the vehicle confirms that it *is* a Hertz rental car. We're getting onto them as I speak, so we should have the victim's name soon. Another bit of good news is that there's an overnight bag in the boot so if we're lucky, we should find out more about the man from the contents.'

The mood around the table definitely improved. Hopefully, once we had the victim's ID, it would be possible to come up with a motive and narrow down the list of suspects. I checked my watch and saw that it was gone one-thirty. Regretfully, I stood up.

'I'm afraid I have to be somewhere else at two-fifteen. If it's okay with you guys, I'll give you a lift back to the villa now and then dash off.' I directed my attention at Marco – after all, this was his case now, even though Virgilio was deeply involved. 'I could come back later on if you need me. Sorry I have to rush off, but I have a client waiting.'

I saw him exchange glances with his boss before answering. 'Thanks a lot, Dan, but you've done your bit already. I'd like to sit down this afternoon and ask the group of six a bit more about who they are and how come people with a potentially criminal background have decided to go into the hotel business. You go off and do what you have to do. You've been a great help with all the interviews, but we should be able to take it from here.' He glanced across at the sergeant. 'I've just discovered that Dini speaks a bit of English so we should be able to cope without you.'

I gave the sergeant a smile. 'That's good to hear. Anyway, if you need me, you know how to contact me.'

On the way out, I picked up one of the restaurant's cards, determined to come back here again with Anna. It had been an excellent meal and probably very good value, although Virgilio had waved away my attempts to pay. I dropped the police officers at the villa and set off again, pleased to have been able to help a little but frustrated that I was having to leave the investigation part way through. Although in my new incarnation as a private investigator, marital infidelity and thieving housemaids were what paid the bills, I couldn't shake off my background in the murder squad.

Fausto Giardino and his wife, Maria, lived towards the top of the range of hills behind my house and Oscar and I knew the roads and tracks around here very well by now. As a result, I had no trouble locating a track leading off their lane into a clump of trees partway between their farmhouse and the main road below. I reversed in and turned off the engine, conscious that there was something I had to do. In case I might have forgotten, one glance in the rear-view mirror told me that Oscar had every intention of ensuring that I didn't forget. It was his lunchtime.

I had only just given him his food bowl when my phone started ringing. A look at my watch told me it was barely five past two, so it looked as though Maria was keen not to be late for her assignation.

But it turned out to be not Fausto, but my daughter, Tricia.

We speak most weeks and in fact we had spoken only a couple of days earlier. As a result, I immediately found myself wondering if there was a special reason for this call.

There was.

'Hi, Dad, all well?'

'I'm fine, thanks, sweetheart, how about you?'

'All good but, listen, I've just had a phone call from Mum. She sounded stressed and she told me she'd seen you. She said something about a murder. Surely the police don't think that she's implicated in anything like that, do they?'

'No, not at all, we were just interviewing all the staff and guests in a hotel close to where a murder took place to see if anybody saw anything or heard anything. To be honest, I thought she looked pretty stressed when I first saw her and I was wondering if she had problems.'

There was a brief pause while Tricia chose her words. 'From what she said, I don't think things are going swimmingly between her and her new man.'

Irrationally, I felt a little wave of pleasure go through me and immediately found myself trying to analyse what was going on inside my head. Was I pleased simply because I hadn't liked the look of Matthew White, the London restaurateur, or was I happy that it looked as though Helen had made a poor decision? Either way, I reminded myself, how she lived her life was no longer my concern, and I already had a wonderful partner in Anna. As tactfully as I could, I asked what the trouble seemed to be, and it soon emerged that Tricia didn't know either.

'The thing is, Dad, it's all been a bit of a whirlwind romance. She only met the man – Matthew, his name is – a month or two ago and I haven't met him yet. I must admit, I was quite surprised when I heard that she was going away with him for a dirty weekend – although it's midweek, you know what I mean.'

I found myself smiling to hear my daughter sounding disapproving of her mother. 'So does this mean that she's maybe discovering that he's not the right man for her?'

'I don't know for sure, but I think so. She sounded a bit confused and definitely upset, so I think something must have happened between them over there in Tuscany, but she wouldn't, or couldn't, tell me.' There was another pause before she came to the crunch. 'I was wondering whether you might be able to give her a call and see what the trouble is? I know it's a bit weird, seeing as you're divorced, but I really think she needs somebody sensible to talk to.'

'And you think I'm sensible?' I was doing my best to keep the conversation light while I mulled over the advisability of contacting my ex-wife. In the end, I took the coward's way out. 'I'm afraid I'm on a job and waiting for a call. Can I ring you later on this afternoon and we'll discuss the best way of handling this? Don't worry, it'll be all right.'

Whether it would or not was a whole other kettle of fish.

7

WEDNESDAY AFTERNOON

The call from Fausto came through barely five minutes later, by which time Oscar and I were sitting in the van digesting our lunch. Needless to say, his had taken a lot less time to consume than mine had.

'She's just set off now down the road towards you. She's in her white 500. You should see her any moment.' Fausto sounded nervous and agitated and I found myself hoping I wouldn't have bad news for him later on.

'Okay, I've got her on the tracker app. Talk later.'

The tracker app was very simple. It had a range of about a kilometre and the closer I was to the back of the vehicle being followed, the louder the bleeping noise became. As the sound reached a crescendo, I saw the little Fiat pass, with Maria at the wheel. She didn't see me so I counted to ten and then pulled out into the lane after her. She was heading down towards the main road where she turned right towards Florence. I followed suit, staying about four or five cars behind. The traffic wasn't too bad and it was quite straightforward to keep her in sight.

The tail ended about twenty minutes later as we were driving along one of the *Lungarni*, the roads that run alongside the mud-coloured River Arno. Maria suddenly indicated left and pulled into the side, squeezing her car into a tight gap in a line of parked cars. As far as I could see, cars were parked nose to tail all the way along the left side of the road ahead of me and I snorted in frustration. The tracker had worked perfectly but if Maria now disappeared into the backstreets of Florence on foot while I was stuck out here in my van, there would be no way I could follow her.

Mercifully, at that moment, I saw a German-registered Mercedes begin to pull out a hundred metres further on and I accelerated like a mad thing to get there before any other car could beat me to the precious parking space. To the considerable annoyance of a flame-red Lancia hard on my heels, I got there first and reversed in, not without difficulty. It was a tight squeeze, but I managed it. I looked back and saw Maria disappearing into a side street, heading into the pedestrians-only *centro storico*, so I hastily opened the boot, Oscar jumped out, and the two of us ran back towards Maria's car where we turned into the narrow street she had taken. At first, I couldn't spot her but just caught sight of her as she overtook a group of slow-moving tourists and disappeared around the corner.

Keeping a discreet distance between us, I followed her through the narrow streets to Piazza della Repubblica, on from there to Piazza del Duomo and around the cathedral's magnificent white, pink and green marble walls. Under other circumstances, it would have been a charming tour of one of the most beautiful cities in the world, but the combined effort of keeping up with Maria – who was clearly in a hurry – and ensuring that Oscar didn't stick his cold, wet nose where he shouldn't among the hordes of tourists, most wearing shorts or short skirts, meant that I had little time for admiring the scenery. From the rear of the cathedral, Maria dived into narrow streets once more before reaching her destination – the famous hospital of Santa Maria Nuova. I stopped and reflected. Could the O in her enigmatic diary entry stand for *Ospedale*? But if so, what about the C?

Maria didn't hesitate. She headed straight for the main entrance and I cursed as I realised that my four-legged friend would bar me from following her inside. But then, as she reached the door and surveyed the signs indicating where the different departments were located, the penny suddenly dropped and all was explained. An arrow to the left pointed to the *Centro Ostetrico,* and without hesitation, Maria headed off towards the obstetrics centre and disappeared. I looked down at Oscar, who was panting in the heat. 'Of course, that's it, Oscar. She's pregnant, that's why she's so happy.'

There seemed little point in lingering here in the direct sunlight for goodness knew how long so I headed back in the direction of the van, hoping I wouldn't find that it had been towed away. I hadn't stopped to check what the parking regulations were on the *Lungarni,* but I knew from expensive personal experience that the parking wardens here didn't muck about. On the way back, I made a quick stop at one of my favourite ice-cream shops and bought a white chocolate and peach cone for me and one of their special dog ice creams on a stick for Oscar. As ever, he didn't take his time and savour his food. He demolished the iced lolly that should have lasted at least ten minutes in less than two, and all the way back to the car, I could see him licking his lips.

When I emerged onto the *Lungarno*, I was relieved to see that my van hadn't been towed away and I stopped to collect the tracker from inside the wheel arch of Maria's car first. When I got to my vehicle, I found it so hot inside after being in the direct sunlight that I had to open all the windows and wait several minutes before either Oscar or I could get in without melting. While waiting, Oscar left his mark on a lamp post to tell other dogs that he now owned the city, and I debated what to do with the news I'd just obtained. It seemed pretty clear to me that Maria had gone to the obstetric unit, and, from the smile on her face, it was a fair assumption that this meant she was pregnant and happy about it. Working on that assumption, I knew that I owed it to her to let her break the exciting news to her husband in person. At the same time, I could imagine Fausto sitting at home desperately waiting to hear my report so, in the end, I opted for obfuscation. I rang his number and it was answered before the second ring.

'*Pronto*, Dan?'

'*Ciao*, Fausto, I have news, and it's very good news. There's absolutely nothing for you to worry about.' I distinctly heard the breath whoosh out of his lungs and I continued. 'I followed Maria to the centre of Florence and I can definitely confirm that she wasn't visiting another man or going anywhere sinister. I feel confident that when she comes home this afternoon, she will have some very good news for you. You just need to be patient for a couple of hours.'

Understandably, he did his best to push me into telling him exactly what I'd seen, but I stood my ground. This sort of news was definitely something a husband should hear from his wife rather than from a private investigator. Finally, although I could tell he was frustrated, he thanked me and the call came to an end. I glanced down at Oscar.

'Love is a many splendoured thing, Oscar…'

He glanced up hopefully but, seeing that I was just waxing poetic and not offering food, he jumped into the back of the car and slumped down with a thud and a heartfelt sigh. I knew how he felt – it had been a busy day.

On my drive back home, I got a phone call from a number I instantly recognised. It was my ex-wife. Doing my best to sound businesslike, I answered.

'Hi, Helen, what can I do for you?'

'Dan, thank goodness.' She sounded decidedly flustered – or worse – and I listened intently, pulling into the side of the road and stopping the engine so that I could concentrate fully on what she had to say as the conversation proceeded. 'I've got myself into a bit of a jam and I need to talk to somebody.'

I tried to sound as reassuring as possible. 'Take your time and just tell me all about it. I'm sure we can find a solution.'

'It's Matt... the man I'm with. There's something wrong.' After the call from Tricia earlier on, this came as no surprise, but I didn't comment, letting Helen tell me in her own words. 'I think there might be something going on and I've got myself caught up in it.'

'What sort of something? You're surely not referring to the murder, are you?'

'No.' She stopped and I gave her time to collect her thoughts before she continued. 'Or maybe yes, I honestly don't know.'

This was sounding distinctly serious, but I tried to keep my tone as calming as possible. 'Just tell me all about it. I'm sure it'll turn out not to be as bad as you think.'

'I'm afraid I didn't tell that inspector the whole truth this morning. When he asked me what I was doing yesterday afternoon, I told him I was at the swimming pool and that's the truth. The trouble is that he then asked me to confirm that Matt had been there as well the whole time and I did, but the fact of the matter is that I can't be completely sure of that. You see, he insisted that we share a bottle of wine over lunch and you know what I'm like after a glass or two of wine; I fell asleep, and I mean real deep sleep for over an hour. When I woke up again, Matt was lying on his sun bed beside me but I have no way of knowing whether he'd been there all the time.'

'That doesn't sound too sinister. What makes you think he might not have been there all the time?'

'When he heard that we were going to be interviewed by the police, he said to me, "Remember to tell them that we were both together all afternoon. You won't forget, will you?" The thing is that if he hadn't said anything, I wouldn't have thought twice about it and of course I would have said that we'd been together.' Her voice deteriorated into little more than a croak. 'But it was the fact that he specifically spoke to me about it that's been worrying me.'

And it was worrying me too. For her boyfriend to say something like that to her was definitely suspicious and it tied in perfectly with the feeling I had got about him maybe not being as honest as he might be. Could it be that Helen had shacked up with a murderer? It was a scary thought but, for now, I tried not to worry her any further.

'Were there other people at the pool at the same time who might have seen what he did and where he went?'

'On and off. It was very hot and most sensible people just came for a quick dip and then disappeared back into the hotel. Matt loves the sun and he insisted that we lie out there. I chose to lie underneath a sun umbrella, although he just stretched out in the bright sunshine. That's the other strange thing. When I woke up, he was still in the direct sunlight but he didn't look red or even a bit darker brown.'

'Which made you think that maybe he hadn't been lying in the sun all the time.'

'Exactly.' There was a pause and when she spoke again, there was embarrassment in her voice. 'Back in the UK, I really thought he was a nice guy, but since coming over here, he's got very tense for some reason.'

'Out of interest, what made you come here to Tuscany? Was it his decision or yours?'

'It was his. It was a last-minute thing – an invite he got from a company he works with for an all-expenses-paid couple of days in the sun. It sounded wonderful, and when he asked me to come, I found it very easy to say yes. I'm now wishing desperately that I'd said no.'

'What sort of company was it that gave him the freebie?'

'Hospitality of some kind. He's in the restaurant business.'

'Where is he now? He's obviously not beside you, because you're talking openly to me.'

'I'm still in the room, but he's not here. I told him I wanted a lie-down and he's gone out for a walk.'

'Are you going to be all right staying there with him or do you want to get away?' For a moment, I found myself considering the nightmare scenario of Helen coming to stay with Anna and me. That would really be too awkward for words – although I had a feeling Anna would have a few choice words to say to me about it. I breathed a little sigh of relief when Helen answered.

'No, I'll be fine. This is our last night here and then tomorrow, we're on the evening plane home.' There was a pause. 'What's going to happen now? Do you have to say something to the inspector, or do we both just forget that this conversation happened?'

The answer to that was simple. I definitely needed to tell Virgilio or Marco but I did my best to answer as diplomatically as possible. 'I know the *commissario*, that's the DCI, very well and I trust him as a police officer and I like him a lot as a friend. I'll talk it over quietly with him and see what he says. I haven't seen him since lunchtime so, for all I know, he may have arrested our murderer by now. Don't worry, your man probably never stirred while you were sleeping.'

'He's not my man.' Probably realising that her reply had come out sounding bitter, she qualified her statement. 'I'll be all right until tomorrow and then when we get back to the UK, I'm going to tell him that I don't think it's working out between us. After all, what he said makes me feel like I can't trust him, and trust is all important.' She hesitated for a moment and then added, 'Whatever your faults, Dan, I knew I could always trust you.'

8

WEDNESDAY LATE AFTERNOON

It was almost five by the time I got back home. Anna had spent the day working in Florence and we had agreed that she would stay down there in her apartment for tonight. This meant I had the evening to myself – and Oscar. I helped myself to a home-made lemonade from the fridge and gave Oscar a big bowl of water – both of us needed to rehydrate after a hot day. I was toying with the idea of walking down to the bar in the village for a cold beer but first I remembered I'd promised to ring my daughter back. I pulled out my phone and called her.

'Hi, Tricia. I've spoken to your mum.'

'How did she sound?'

I gave her a brief summary of the conversation, leaving out what Matthew White had said to Helen about their time by the pool and just saying that I had the impression things weren't working out between them. When I mentioned that it sounded as though the relationship was on its last legs, Tricia's reaction was one of relief.

'I think that's very sensible of her. I've been doing a little bit of

online research this afternoon about Matthew White and I'm not
sure I'm too happy about what I've been reading.'

'In what way?'

'His father moved over from Sicily in the 1960s and opened
his first restaurant in Clapham. His name was Alfonso Bianchi
and when he got British citizenship, he changed his surname to
White – that's a direct translation, isn't it?'

'Just because his dad changed his name doesn't mean
anything sinister.' I thought I'd better play this down, although
mention of Sicily inevitably stirred up thoughts of organised
crime. What Tricia said next made me sit up and pay close
attention.

'Of course, but it's not that. The father was obviously a go-
ahead businessman and he set up eight restaurants all over
London, including his flagship restaurant in Soho. When he died
five years ago, Matthew inherited the lot but I don't think he has
the business acumen of his father, and two of the restaurants
have recently closed. Both restaurants were involved in a scandal
two years ago and they never recovered.'

'What sort of scandal?'

'Serving substandard food, I believe. A load of people got
food poisoning. There are lots of comments on the Internet
about it.'

I couldn't help thinking of Fausto's cat salami story but I
didn't mention it to Tricia. 'That's interesting – maybe he's having
money troubles.'

'I don't know if Matthew's in financial trouble, but, if he is, I
hope he doesn't think he can get Mum to bail him out.' Helen's
parents had been very well off and, when her mother had died a
year ago, according to Tricia, Helen had inherited a tidy sum.

I decided to play down any possible criminal activity by
Helen's boyfriend here in Tuscany but I knew I would definitely

be passing on this information to Virgilio. 'Who knows? At least, from what your mum said, it sounds as though she's about to dump him, so that problem shouldn't crop up.'

'Are you going to see Mum before she comes home tomorrow?'

'I asked her if she was happy to stay at the hotel with him for tonight or if she needed rescuing, and she said she's happy to stay. So, no, I won't be seeing her again.'

And I was glad about that. Although Helen had been looking good and sounding friendly, I knew I would never forget the final months of our failed marriage when her attitude towards me and my work had been very different. She had been very bitter, accusing me – probably correctly – of caring more about policing than I did about her. The irony that she was now coming to me, the detective, for help, wasn't lost on me.

Half an hour later, as Oscar and I were walking down to the bar in the village, I received a phone call from Virgilio. I'd called to relay the information about Matthew White's restaurant scandal, but it had gone to voicemail and I'd left a message for him to call me back.

'*Ciao*, Dan, you called? I need to speak to you anyway. We're going to need your help again if you can spare the time.'

My ears pricked up and I stopped in the shade of a hundred-year-old cypress tree. Oscar wandered over and squeezed into the shade at my feet, tongue hanging out. 'Of course, I'm happy to help. What's new?'

'We now have the identity of the victim and he was one of yours: a Brit. Hertz sent us a copy of his driving licence and his name's Anthony Greenbank, he was thirty-six, and he lived in London. But the interesting thing we found while checking on his background is that he was a journalist. This means he was probably over here on the trail of something shady.'

'Who did he work for? Was he with a newspaper or other media outlet of some sort?'

'We're still looking into it, and hopefully, you can help us as well with your contacts in London, but his profile on Twitter or whatever it's called nowadays says that he was an independent investigative journalist.'

'That's a pity. If he was working for a big media company, almost certainly his editor would have been able to tell us why he came here and the name of the person he was investigating. If he was an independent, he might have been keeping his cards close to his chest. I'll certainly get onto it. I don't suppose there was a laptop or a phone in the car by any chance?'

'Alas no, and no sign of a wallet or passport. Thanks, Dan, it'll be very helpful if you can do a bit of digging, and what would be even more helpful would be if you could spare a couple of hours tomorrow morning. Given that the victim was a British journalist, it's quite likely that his target was also British. What I'd like to do is to interview all the Brits and anybody you and Marco found suspicious at the hotel one more time tomorrow morning to find out a bit more about each of them. It goes without saying that almost anybody staying there must be very well off and quite possibly some of them may be spending dirty money. Who knows? Could you spare me the time?'

'Of course. Shall I come to the hotel at nine like today?'

'Terrific, thanks. What about you? Did you have something you wanted to tell me?'

'It's probably nothing, but I've discovered that Matthew White, the English guy that Marco and I didn't like the look of, was involved with a scandal after two of his restaurants gave a load of people food poisoning. The restaurants have now closed, but it might mean that White's prepared to cut corners and he might need money. There's something else that may mean nothing at all, but maybe you could ask the *Antimafia* people in Rome to check on him just in case, as I've discovered he has Sicilian roots. His father moved to the UK and changed the family name from Bianchi to White after getting UK citizenship. I'll give Paul at Scotland Yard a call and ask him if he knows anything. As I say, there may be nothing in it, but I think it's worth checking.'

'It's definitely worth checking. Thanks.'

Down at the bar, I ran into a number of regulars, among them my friend Giovanni, the postman and font of all knowledge about Montevolpone and its surroundings. It came as little surprise to find myself questioned by him on events at the hotel.

'I gather there's been a murder at the Podere dei Santi and I've heard that you've been helping the police. Is it true that the guy was held down while a truck drove over him?'

Even though I knew him well by now, it still amazed me how Giovanni managed to get his information, although it was almost a relief to hear that he hadn't got all his facts straight this time. I decided to tell him the bare minimum and try to see what else he might have heard.

'Your spies are right, Giovanni, I have been helping the police, but just with some interpreting, seeing as a number of the guests at the hotel speak English. I gather the body wasn't found at the villa but down by the winery.'

'Are you sure the guy wasn't killed by Guido's dog?'

'Guido?'

'Guido Renzi, he works at the winery and he's got one of the nastiest dogs I've ever come across – and as a postman, I see my fair share of hostile dogs.'

I remembered the aggressive mongrel and I also remembered his uncommunicative owner. 'How come you know him – the man rather than the dog? And, no, as far as I know, the dog is innocent of murder.'

'A couple of years back, I had to cover for a colleague from the sorting office in Montespertoli who was off sick. I was there for four months and I got to know Guido at the winery pretty well because I used to stop off most mornings for a coffee with Auntie Linda.'

It was like hearing a spy revealing his sources. 'And Auntie Linda works at the winery or the hotel?'

He shook his head. 'Neither, she lives in the little cottage directly opposite the winery. She found the body yesterday.'

'And she told you?'

'No, she told Vittorio, who told Bartolomeo, who told me.'

I didn't even try to find out the identity of Giovanni's string of contacts and I marvelled yet again at his ability to obtain and retain information. 'Was she the person who told you the man had been held down while the truck drove over him?'

'No, that's what Guido told his wife. She's the hairdresser here and she told my wife.' I had often thought that Giovanni would be better employed as a spymaster so I didn't even query this new information chain, but he hadn't finished yet. 'Auntie Linda, well, she's really Great-Aunt Linda, told my wife when she phoned earlier that she'd been visited by a man with a funny accent and a big, black dog. She said he was asking questions like a policeman.'

Trying not to dwell on this scathing indictment of my linguistic prowess, I gave up and told him the truth – or at least a version of it. 'Okay, so I was asking a few questions this morning, but I've left it to the police now and I've been in Florence all afternoon. What I can tell you is that the victim certainly wasn't held down as the truck drove over him. From what the police said, he was already dead when he ended up in the road.'

Giovanni nodded a couple of times. 'Better like that, poor devil. Any idea who he was and why he was killed?'

I wasn't going to reveal anything more about the inquiry so I pleaded ignorance. 'By the sound of it, you know more about it than I do. Tell me, do you or your friends have any theories as to who might have done it?'

'I've been wondering about that. Mancini, who runs the winery, treats his staff like dirt and Auntie Linda's scared stiff of him. Although she rents her cottage from the American, Mancini acts as though he's the landlord, and she has to put up with a lot of noise and disruption, sometimes late at night. She says she doesn't dare complain because she's scared Mancini will throw her out.'

I shook my head disapprovingly. 'Not a nice man, by the sound of it.'

'No, he certainly isn't. Up at the hotel, they're all pretty good – I'm talking about the staff – although Nando, the chef, has a terrible temper or so they say. But what about the guests? Could one of them have done it?'

'I have no idea. Maybe when the police find out more about the victim, they'll get some leads.'

At that moment, Giovanni's phone buzzed and he jumped to his feet. 'See you, Dan. That's my wife telling me she needs me at home. She sounds as if she's in a bit of a mood so I'd better go.'

Moments later, Tommaso, the barista, appeared and took my order of a cold beer for me and a bowl of water for Oscar. When the drinks arrived, I finally sat back and relaxed. It had been a long day.

9

WEDNESDAY EVENING

But the day wasn't over yet.

When I got back home at just after seven, I heard a vehicle outside and glanced out of the window to see a blue pickup pull into my yard. At the wheel was Fausto Giardino and when he saw me at the window, he waved to me to come outside. I did as requested, hoping that he hadn't come to tell me his wife hadn't said anything about her afternoon assignation, but the smile on his face soon allayed my fears.

'*Ciao*, Dan. I've come to say thank you.' He fended off a boisterous greeting from Oscar. 'Maria told me everything, and I'm the happiest man in the world. She's known for some weeks now, but she didn't want to say anything until she was completely sure. We've been trying for so long, she didn't want to build my hopes up and then disappoint me. The people at the obstetrics unit in Florence have confirmed that she's definitely expecting, and it's all looking good.' His expression became a bit more remorseful. 'I shouldn't have doubted her. I've been so stupid.'

I went over and clapped him on the shoulder. 'All's well that

ends well, Fausto. Congratulations to you both. We need to cele-
brate. Come in and have a glass of wine.'

He pointed to the back of the pickup. 'That sounds like a
great idea, but the wine is on me.'

I followed the direction of his pointing finger and saw a *dami-
giana* sitting in the truck. These massive, fifty-litre, onion-shaped
glass bottles in protective straw casings like huge Chianti flasks
were familiar to me by now. Like many Italians, I now tended to
buy my wine in bulk and bottle it myself.

'Give me a hand, Dan. This is for you. Just a little thank you.'

'A *little* thank you?' I protested, but he was adamant, and
together, we hefted the heavy container off the truck and carried
it into the house. After squeezing it onto the floor of the larder,
we toasted the forthcoming happy event with a bottle of
spumante from my fridge.

It was almost eight by the time he left, pumping my hand
gratefully and still looking absolutely delighted. After he'd
driven off, I cut myself a few slices of ham – as usual, the first
slice going to Oscar – and sat down to an immensely satisfying
cold dinner of bread, ham, melon and fresh goat's cheese from
the shepherd up the road. With a glass or two of Fausto's father's
wine from last year, it was an excellent meal and the fact that I
knew the names of everybody responsible for what was on my
table was a great feeling. Yes, I go to the supermarket every now
and then for toilet rolls and washing powder, but most of what I
eat is locally sourced. I couldn't say the same about my time in
London when half my meals – especially in the final years of my
marriage – had been takeaways. Thought of my abortive
marriage made me think of Helen and the murder yet again.

On the walk back up from the village, I had phoned Inspector
Paul Wilson, my former colleague at Scotland Yard, and asked if

he could dig up anything on Anthony Greenbank. From time to time, Paul helps me with cases involving Brits, and he promised to see what he could do. While I was at it, I asked him to check Matthew White as well.

I had also phoned my good friend Jess Barnes in London. She is a journalist who greatly helped me by writing a review of *Death Amid the Vines*, my first attempt at a murder mystery. Although I enjoy working as Dan Armstrong, Private Investigator, I have always had a hankering to become an author, and this new career was now starting to take off. I'd been lucky enough to get a deal with a British publisher, but the full-page article that Jess had somehow got into *The Sunday Times* colour supplement had provided an amazing boost to sales when the book had come out in the spring. I asked her if she knew the name Anthony Greenbank, and, although it didn't ring any bells, she said that she would do a bit of digging and get back to me if she had any news.

I was still trying to work out what had brought a British journalist to my part of rural Tuscany and I determined to search the Internet after dinner for any reference to him in the hope of discovering his secret. As for Helen, having told Tricia that I wouldn't be seeing her mother again, it now looked as though I would indeed see her next morning for the second round of interviews and I had mixed feelings as far as that was concerned.

After thirty years of marriage, the divorce had come as a brutal blow to me, and it had taken me many months before I'd managed to convince myself that I was better off without her. I had actively sought to forget her and then, of course, almost a year ago, I had met Anna and my life had changed. She and I had bonded immediately and I was happy and comfortable with her – and as far as I could tell, she was similarly happy with me. Now, suddenly, here I was, faced with the woman who had divorced me and broken my heart, but I somehow still felt strangely protective towards her in spite of what had happened. What did this say about me? I talked it over with Oscar but he wasn't much help. He's an excellent listener – something Helen often accused me of not being – but he doesn't contribute much to the conversation.

My musings were interrupted by my phone. It was Anna, and as soon as I heard her voice, a wave of guilt swept over me, almost as though I had been unfaithful. As the conversation proceeded, it turned out I was right to feel guilty, but this had nothing to do with my ex-wife.

'*Ciao*, Dan, how's it going?' She didn't sound very interested, and I wondered if there might be something bothering her.

'I'm fine, thanks. I'm pleased to report that I've solved Fausto's problem and he's riotously happy as a result.' I didn't tell her the nature of the problem or its solution and she didn't ask. Like I say, I try to keep business and pleasure at arm's length. So why was she sounding downbeat? I tried a bit of gentle digging. 'All well with you?'

She ignored the question. 'And what about the murder at the hotel? I suppose you've solved that one as well.' I could tell from her indifferent tone that she wasn't happy and I struggled to think what I might have done to upset her.

'Not yet, but we've just discovered that the victim was a British journalist. Virgilio called earlier. He wants me to go back there again in the morning for more interviews while he and Marco try to work out if there's somebody there with a suspicious past.'

'What sort of suspicious past?' She still didn't sound best pleased and, again, I wondered why. Surely she couldn't have found out about Helen, could she?

'No idea – drugs, fraud, maybe even murder. Who knows? By

the way, we went to a lovely restaurant for lunch and I hope you'll let me take you there. What are you doing tomorrow?'

'Oh, Dan.' She suddenly sounded a whole lot happier. 'So you *have* remembered. Do you want me to drive out and meet you there?'

Remembered what? It took me a few more seconds before the truth dawned on me. Today was the fourteenth and tomorrow would be the fifteenth of September, Anna's birthday. I had remembered a week or two ago and had even bought her a bracelet as a present as well as promising to take her out for a slap-up lunch, but with all the excitement of a murder investigation, it had slipped my mind. Whether this was simply to do with pressure of work or the onset of dementia was debatable, but I wasn't going to wrestle with that now. I hastily did a bit of damage limitation.

'I've been trying to work out where's best for us to go. I'll make sure I've finished at the hotel by mid or late morning so I can easily come down and pick you up from your place. We could go somewhere in Florence if you prefer, or there's that lovely old restaurant in Lastra a Signa.'

'We went there only last month. Let's try your new find. Apart from anything else, it might be a bit cooler out there in the country. Today's been really clammy. I know, I'll drive out and meet you at the hotel. I've never been there and I'd like to take a look at it.'

'Well, if you're sure. Shall we meet at noon?'

We chatted some more before she wished me goodnight and the call ended. At least by that time, she was sounding a lot happier, but the same could not be said for me. The realisation had been dawning on me in the course of the conversation that having my current partner and my ex-wife in the same place at the same time could be potentially explosive. I laid the phone back on the table, took a big mouthful of wine and addressed my slumbering dog.

'What would you do, Oscar? Should I phone her back and tell her what's happened, or do I just keep my fingers crossed that the two of them don't cross paths tomorrow?'

One eye opened and the end of his tail wagged weakly before he relapsed into a comatose state once again. I gave it a few more seconds and then decided to follow his example and weasel out. After all, Helen and Anna had never met before, so there was no reason they would recognise each other, even if they were to meet. I decided I wouldn't say anything to Anna and I would do my very best to ensure that I was waiting outside the hotel at midday tomorrow so I could whisk her away to the porcupine restaurant before she was able to meet my ex. I knew I was taking a chance, but it seemed preferable to making a difficult phone call tonight. I could only hope it would all turn out all right.

At the end of my meal, I dug out the card I had picked up at the restaurant and called to book a table for two for the following lunchtime. After that, I grabbed my iPad and went outside, hoping that the mosquitoes wouldn't be out in force tonight. It was almost completely dark now, although the distant western horizon was still glowing red. I sat down and plumbed Anthony Greenbank into the search engine. Over the course of the next hour and a half, I viewed every entry I could find about the man and came away slightly wiser but still without a clue as to what had brought him here to Tuscany.

'Ant' Greenbank had studied journalism at the University of Leeds before getting a job as a cub reporter at the *Yorkshire Evening Post*. After three years there, he had headed for the capital where he'd worked for the *Metro* and the *Evening Standard*. His big break had come in 2016 when he got a job with the *Sunday Express* and I found a number of pieces by him on subjects as varied as drug addiction, Brexit (inevitably) and post-natal depression. As far as I could tell, he had been freelance for five years now – whether this was by choice or economic pressures in the media industry remained unclear.

I found a number of articles with his name on them since then – most in the *Sunday Express* and the *Daily Mail*, but also in half a dozen other papers. As the years had passed, so his articles had become more prominent and the most recent had occupied a double-page spread in *The Mail on Sunday* colour supplement. This one dealt with holiday rental companies ripping off unsuspecting tourists, and most of the other articles also dealt with fraud of some description. On that basis, I was tempted to think that he had probably come here on the trail of a fraudster, and it would be our job tomorrow to see if we could come up with somebody at the hotel who fell into that category.

Although I tended to share Virgilio's opinion that it was most likely that Greenbank's target had been a fellow Brit, the three Italian 'businessmen' with their bodyguards would definitely merit closer investigation. Hopefully, by tomorrow, Virgilio's contacts in Rome would have been able to provide a bit more information about their true nature.

It was after ten by the time I switched off the iPad and gave Oscar a gentle nudge with my toe. 'Feel like a little walk?'

Of course he did.

We went out and followed the *strada bianca* up the hill, the white gravel making it easy for me to keep tabs on Oscar, although he's usually pretty good and he tends to stay close to me. Of course, the appearance of a squirrel would have seen him charge off into the undergrowth without a backward glance, but at this time of night, they were hopefully all tucked up in bed. As I walked, I was still turning over two problems in my head: the murder of the journalist, and Anna. I didn't feel right about lying to her – or at least omitting to tell her about having bumped into Helen – so I gradually came to the conclusion that I owed it to her to reveal all, but I felt that this should be face to face, rather than on the phone. The best time to do that would be at lunch the following day. Hopefully, it wouldn't put her off what promised to be a very good meal and if all went well, she might appreciate my honesty.

I was just starting to think about the murder again when my phone started ringing. It was Paul at Scotland Yard.

'Hi, Paul, are you on the night shift tonight?'

'Hi, Dan. No, just working late. I'm off home soon but I wanted to give you a heads-up on Anthony Greenbank first. His name came up on the system. He filed a complaint only a couple of weeks ago about threats he'd been receiving from an anonymous email address. It says here that he was a journalist, but you probably know that already, and he's been investigating some international fraudsters. He was unable or unwilling to name names and our people couldn't do much about it apart from log it. I don't suppose that helps you too much. He lived alone, so there's nobody close to him who might have more information about what he was doing over there.'

'Thanks for that, Paul. I'll tell the police here and I'm sure they'll be equally grateful. Any joy with Matthew White and the food poisoning?'

'Nothing on the system, but one of the guys here told me he remembers reading about a scandal a few years back about him selling salami made with hedgehog or some such, but there was no criminal case.'

I felt a flash of disappointment. After what White had said to Helen by the pool, I'd been hoping Paul would have been able to turn up a history of violent crime indicating that White might have been our murderer, but such was not the case. As for the 'hedgehog' sausage, this was a slight improvement on cat, but not a lot. I thanked Paul very much and we chatted briefly before he hung up, leaving me pensive. Time was tight and I was acutely aware that the hotel guests would be clamouring to leave. And, of course, they included my ex-wife and Matthew White, purveyor of tainted meat.

10

THURSDAY MORNING

Next day, my early-morning walk with Oscar was interrupted by my phone. I checked the time as I answered it and saw that it was ten to eight. It was the recently promoted Inspector Marco Innocenti.

'*Ciao*, Marco. Are you up early or still awake from last night?'

'A bit of both. I've just taken a call from the Podere dei Santi. There's been another murder, this time at the hotel.'

'Another death? Who is it this time?'

'It's Luigi Bellomo from Naples, one of the three "business-men" allegedly here to buy a villa and turn it into a hotel.'

This came as a considerable surprise. To have two murders in the same area in two days was unusual to say the least, and in all probability, they had to be linked in some way. Had Anthony Greenbank been investigating Bellomo and/or his companions, but, if so, why had Bellomo ended up dead as well? 'I presume you're going up there now. Virgilio called me last night and we arranged that I would go to the hotel this morning to interview the English speakers again. I'll be with you by nine.'

'Thanks, Dan, that's good of you.'

After a quick walk and a hasty shower, I grabbed a cup of coffee, gave a slice of bread to Oscar, picked up a croissant for myself and headed out to the van with him. We made good time and arrived at the hotel at a quarter to nine to find no fewer than five police cars already parked outside and uniformed officers moving amid the vines, clearly looking for something. I spotted Sergeant Dini standing by the front door and hurried across.

'Morning, Sergeant, what's new?'

'Good morning, sir... Dan. The body of Bellomo was found by the groundsman just down there in the vineyard, and the inspector has got people out looking for the other missing person.'

'*Another* missing person? Who's that?'

'Achille Calabrese from Milan, one of Bellomo's companions.'

I stood in silence for a few moments while I digested that information. It didn't make sense. Assuming Greenbank had been spying on them and had been eliminated for his trouble, why had one or maybe even two of his targets been murdered? Alternatively, maybe Calabrese had murdered Bellomo – and maybe Anthony Greenbank as well – and had now done a runner. I couldn't get my head around it and I could see from the sergeant's expression that she was having trouble with it as well.

At that moment, Marco appeared at the door and came across to shake hands.

'*Ciao*, Dan, thanks for coming so quickly. Has Dini filled you in? It seems there might be another victim – either that or Calabrese's done a disappearing act. His Ferrari's still in the car park so we're searching all around the area now and I've got people inside checking the hotel, room by room.'

'What about the third conspirator? What was his name... Cassano, wasn't it? Is he still here and alive?'

Marco nodded. 'Alive and very worried. He's as white as a

sheet, and it's pretty clear he's afraid he's going to be the next victim.'

I tried to sound encouraging. 'Well, hopefully if he's scared stiff, he'll be prepared to tell us what on earth's going on, even if it's just to save his skin.'

Our conversation was interrupted by the sound of a shout from the vineyard. Leaving the sergeant at the front door, Marco and I set off at a run with Oscar charging along with us, convinced that this was a game. What we found when we reached the end of a row of vines, less than fifty metres from the hotel car park, was anything but a game. I reached down to catch hold of Oscar's collar but, seasoned trooper that he was by now, he immediately stopped and remained rooted to the spot, so as not to compromise the crime scene. In front of us, the body of a man was splayed face down on the ground, and you didn't need to be a forensic pathologist to see the cause of death. Massive trauma to the back of his head indicated that he'd received a powerful blow from behind. Marco turned to the officer who had found the body, a young man whose face was currently the colour of the gravel at his feet.

'Alfieri, stay here and don't let anybody near the body until Forensics have had a chance to examine it.' Marco pointed down at the dusty earth. 'There are footprints here that might provide us with evidence.' He laid his hand on the constable's shoulder for a second or two. 'I know it's not a pretty sight but he's dead, and there's nothing we can do about it now.'

The officer nodded, collected himself, and even managed to produce a salute in response. I stood there and studied the body closely. The victim was fully dressed and I could see a bulge in his back pocket indicating the presence of either a wallet or a phone. There was an expensive-looking Rolex on his wrist, so that appeared to eliminate robbery as a motive. Taking care not to tread too close to the body, Marco squatted down to study the man's face at close quarters and confirmed that this was indeed Achille Calabrese. The fact that two of the three mysterious 'businessmen' had been killed in one night was surely not a coincidence, and my thoughts returned to the third man, Cassano, who potentially held the key to what had been going on here. Of course, there were also the three bodyguards who, quite plainly, had been seriously negligent – or worse. I hoped I would be invited to sit in on their interviews.

The sound of a siren told us that Virgilio's Alfa Romeo had just arrived, and Marco and I returned to the front door to find him deep in conversation with Sergeant Dini. He shook hands with both of us and told us that he brought news. 'I've heard back from the *Antimafia* people again and what they say is interesting – although if we'd heard yesterday, we might have been able to stop the murder of Luigi Bellomo.'

Marco interrupted him with the news that the body of Achille Calabrese had also been found now and Virgilio shook his head in disbelief before turning his attention to me. 'Two of them murdered? Tell me, Dan, have you heard of the SCU?'

I shook my head and took a guess. 'A trade union maybe?'

'A lot nastier than that. The initials stand for *Sacra Corona Unita*, the sacred united crown, and it's often been referred to as the "Fourth Mafia" along with the *Camorra*, *'Ndrangheta* and *Cosa Nostra*. It started life in southern Italy, principally Puglia, and for a while, it expanded across the whole country and into parts of Europe. Fortunately, a lot of its members were arrested and jailed in the early two thousands and, although it's still in business, it's more as a loose collection of criminal gangs nowadays.'

'I see, and the connection with what's been going on here?'

'*Antimafia* have unearthed the fact that Bellomo, Calabrese and Cassano are all originally from Puglia and apparently there's been talk down there of trying to revive the SCU as a more powerful criminal organisation to rival the *Camorra*, *'Ndrangheta*, or the Sicilian Mafia. Rome thinks there could be a good chance that our three characters met up here in great secrecy to do just that.'

Marco had been following his boss carefully. 'So the fact that two of them have been killed would appear to indicate that their secret plan wasn't so secret after all, and somebody didn't like what they were planning.'

Virgilio nodded. 'Exactly, and presumably the English journalist got wind of what was happening and was eliminated either by the three plotters and their bodyguards or by a hitman sent from Puglia to get rid of them.'

I shook my head slowly. 'I can see the logic of what you're saying about the Puglia connection, but it amazes me that a British journalist could have discovered what was going on. Still, at least we're a bit closer to knowing why these people have been killed.' I caught Virgilio's eye. 'I suppose next on the agenda is a serious talk with Signor Cassano?'

'Yes, indeed. I think all three of us will want to take part in that, don't you?'

I nodded eagerly. 'I'd be fascinated to hear what this guy has to say for himself.'

'Well, come on, then, let's go and see him. Where is he now, Dini?'

She didn't need to consult her clipboard. 'Barricaded in room twenty-seven with two police officers outside the door.'

'And the bodyguards? Not that they've done a lot of good.'

'In their rooms under guard as well.'

'Excellent. Right, let's go and see Signor Cassano.'

* * *

Room twenty-seven was on the second floor and a sign on the door described it as the *Apennine Suite*. Clearly, money had been no object for these men. The police officers on the landing outside the room let the four of us in and closed the door firmly behind us. The interior was predictably luxurious with a living room and a separate bedroom as well as a bathroom. Sitting in the living room with a blanket around his shoulders was a demoralised-looking Davide Cassano, a half-empty bottle of whisky and a glass on the table in front of him. He looked up nervously as he heard us come in and then returned his attention to his knees. He was strongly built and I'd been told that he was around my age, although today, his face was wracked with anguish and he looked older. Interestingly, Oscar, who can normally tell when somebody's unhappy, made no move towards him and I mentally chalked that up as a bad mark for Cassano.

Virgilio placed a voice recorder on the table in front of Cassano, pressed Record and started the interview.

'Your name is Davide Cassano?'

'Yes.' The man nodded but didn't look up or make any other comment.

'You live in Bari?'

'Yes.'

'You came here with your two companions, Luigi Bellomo and Achille Calabrese?' There was barely a hint of a nod of the head and Virgilio carried on. 'I'm sorry to have to tell you that the bodies of both your companions have been found outside in the vineyard. They've been murdered.'

This news finally galvanised Cassano into action. He looked up, and the expression on his face was one of unbridled terror. 'Both dead? How were they killed? Have you caught whoever it was who did this?'

Marco answered. 'Both were struck with a heavy instrument

on the back of the head and the impact crushed the skull.' I could tell that Marco was laying it on a bit thick so as to increase the man's stress levels and, hopefully, his willingness to talk. 'As for the perpetrators, we're following a number of leads.' This was stretching the truth but I didn't blame Marco for a bit of embellishment.

Virgilio continued. 'We fear that your life may well be in danger as well, Signor Cassano. If we're to protect you, we need to know from whom. Tell me, who do *you* think is responsible for killing your two friends?'

Cassano looked up and, for a moment, it looked as though he was about to speak up but, in the end, all he did was shake his head and mumble, 'I have no idea.'

Virgilio hardened his voice. 'Two of your friends have been brutally murdered and you have no idea who might have done it? Try a bit harder, Signor Cassano.'

'I've told you, I don't know.'

'You'll be safe with us, you know.'

This drew no response and Virgilio and I exchanged looks.

Since moving to Italy, I'd heard of the Mafia code of *omertà*, the pledge to maintain silence when questioned about the criminal organisation. It was fascinating, if incredible, to see it in action. This man was clearly petrified that he would end up suffering the same fate as his two companions but, even though the police were offering to protect him, he still refused to speak up. Of course, I had also heard the stories that Italian prisons were infiltrated by and in some cases effectively run by the Mafia, so presumably he knew that if he did decide to talk and admitted being part of the SCU, he would end up spending time in prison. If that were to happen, I had little doubt that he would be found dead in his cell sooner rather than later. Better to say nothing, plead ignorance and hope for the best.

I didn't envy him.

Virgilio returned to more practical matters. 'Please can you tell me what you were doing last night from when you finished your dinner onwards?'

'I'd been having discussions with Bellomo and Calabrese all day yesterday and we went out onto the terrace after dinner and continued. That would have been about ten o'clock.'

'And your other three "companions" – you and I both know they're bodyguards – what about them?'

'They came out with us and sat on a separate table a little distance from us. Our discussions are highly confidential.'

Virgilio gave him a sceptical look. 'But not confidential enough, by the look of it. And what time did you go to bed?'

'Well after midnight. The bar closed at twelve but the waiter brought us a bottle of wine and we carried on talking for a while. I suppose I was in bed by one or so.'

'And the others?'

'I have no idea. To be honest, Bellomo and Calabrese had been hitting the bottle pretty hard all day and I left them looking a bit the worse for wear. For all I know, they might have fallen asleep at the table.'

'And the three bodyguards?'

'Rossini came up with me, but I've no idea about the others. I imagine they stayed with Bellomo and Calabrese.'

The interview continued for a further ten minutes, during which Cassano probably only spoke a couple of dozen more words, mainly, 'No' or 'I don't know'. Finally, Virgilio gave up and we left room twenty-seven to discuss our findings on the landing. Needless to say, we all felt the same way: deeply frustrated. Marco put it into words for the four of us.

'I don't know about you, but I'm in absolutely no doubt that Cassano and the other two were plotting some sort of takeover, and somebody in the SCU sent a hitman or a hit squad to kill them. The trouble is that we're going to get no help from the man who could be the next victim.'

Virgilio nodded. 'Exactly, I've seen it so many times. We know he's deeply implicated, but he also knows that we can't prove it. There's no way he's going to give us any clues to help us trace the killer or killers, so it looks like we've hit a dead end as far as he's concerned.'

I added a bit of encouragement. 'I agree that it looks as though we're on a hiding to nothing with Cassano, but we've still got the three bodyguards. You never know, one of them may be prepared to talk – or one of them may even be the killer.'

Virgilio nodded. 'I really hope they talk, but I have my doubts.' He turned to the sergeant. 'Where are the bodyguards, Dini?'

'Rooms twenty-two, twenty-four and twenty-six.' She pointed at the door directly across the corridor from us with the number twenty-six on it. 'Would you like to start here?' She consulted her clipboard. 'Salvatore Rossini, age forty-eight, also from Bari, bodyguard to Cassano.'

Virgilio grunted. 'At least his employer's still breathing, which is more than can be said for the other two.'

11

THURSDAY MORNING

Salvatore Rossini stood up when we came into his room and I could see that, although he wasn't very tall, he was powerfully built. The immediate thought that sprang into my head was that he would probably have had no problem coercing the victims into the vines and then doing away with them.

This was another fine room but considerably smaller than the suite across the corridor, so we all remained standing while Virgilio began the questioning, asking the man to confirm his name and his address in Bari. When Rossini spoke, I had great difficulty in understanding everything he said, partly because he had a strong southern-Italian accent and partly because he was one of those people whose gravelly voices make them barely audible. I kept a close eye on him and didn't immediately see any signs of guilt, but I saw few signs of cooperation either. Virgilio didn't beat about the bush.

'At least you still have a job, Signor Rossini – unlike your companions. Tell me, why do you think Signor Cassano is still alive and the other two dead? Is it because you're such a good bodyguard or is it just chance?'

Rossini looked up at him in what appeared to be genuine surprise – either that or he was a good actor. 'What do you mean? I heard that Bellomo had been killed but I thought Calabrese had just gone off.'

'I regret to inform you that we've also found the body of Achille Calabrese, his skull smashed in just like Luigi Bellomo.'

Rossini looked appalled. 'Both dead?'

Virgilio left him standing there in silence for a few moments before addressing him again. 'I imagine you'll agree that it's a fair assumption that Cassano, Bellomo and Calabrese each engaged the services of a bodyguard because they were afraid that something might happen to them. It has now happened to two of the three. I'll ask you again: why is your boss still alive? Is it because you're such a talented bodyguard or for some other reason?'

Rossini shook his head. 'I have no idea. Look, I was employed to keep an eye on Signor Cassano but that's as much as I know.'

'Do you feel like hazarding a guess? Was he afraid of a jealous husband maybe?' The irony in Virgilio's voice was only too clear.

'Who knows? All three were wealthy men, and money brings enemies, doesn't it?'

'How did they get their money?'

'Don't ask me, I was just brought along for protection. Nobody told me anything.'

It was clear by now that either he had nothing to tell us or, more probably, that he knew plenty but he wasn't going to give anything away. Virgilio asked him where he'd been between dinner and breakfast and the answer was what his boss had told us about going out on the terrace after dinner until well after midnight. He had then seen Cassano safely into his suite, after which he'd crossed the corridor to his room at 1 a.m. and gone to sleep. He had no knowledge of what the others had done, but he corroborated Cassano's story that the other two 'big fish' – now defunct – had been very drunk. Finally, Virgilio told him not to leave the hotel until he got permission from the police, and Rossini smiled.

'As long as Signor Cassano's paying, that's fine by me.'

Outside in the corridor, our mood was gloomy. It looked as though we weren't going to get any more out of the bodyguards than we had from Cassano. Nevertheless, Marco sounded a note of optimism all the same.

'At least we now know that both victims were outside between midnight and one, and quite possibly a whole lot longer than that. As far as the murderer was concerned, that made them sitting ducks.'

'But only if their bodyguards left their posts or got together to murder them.'

Virgilio's phone started ringing and his expression brightened as he listened to the incoming news. When the call ended, he told us what he'd heard.

'That was Gianni from the morgue. He's going to do autopsies on Bellomo and Calabrese as soon as he gets back to Florence, and he says his people are taking casts of shoeprints around where the bodies were found in the vineyard. The same type of ribbed sole appears at both crime scenes so it looks as though they may have both been killed by a single perpetrator, one after the other. Time of death for both is provisionally between midnight and 3 a.m., which fits in nicely with the time the victims were last seen outside on the terrace. From there to where the bodies were found is barely a hundred metres. As soon as we have copies of the casts – Gianni will send photos – we need to search the rooms belonging to Cassano and the three bodyguards in the hope of finding a match. You never know, we might get lucky.'

I felt I had to comment. 'But how on earth did a single perpetrator manage to get the victims to walk into the vineyard so they could be murdered? However drunk they were, that seems complicated, not least as the two bodyguards were allegedly sitting right beside them. Of course, the bodyguards may have been working together and taken one victim each but you say there's only one set of footprints alongside each victim. Maybe they suggested a late-night walk or they went into the vines to answer a call of nature.' A thought occurred to me. 'By the way, any joy with the CCTV footage? I don't suppose there's a camera on the terrace.'

This time, it was the sergeant who answered. 'I've just had a text from our tech people who're studying the footage. There's no sign of any of the six exiting the hotel by the front door after lunch on Tuesday afternoon when the Englishman was killed. There's a camera at the back door looking out over the terrace and the pool, but it was out of commission. It's being fixed as we speak. This means that any one of them could have gone out that way to murder the journalist on Tuesday afternoon without being seen, and the same applies to last night's murders. We have no footage at all of what happened out on the terrace.'

I couldn't help thinking that this meant that my ex-wife's boyfriend could easily have slipped away from the pool on Tuesday afternoon unobserved and murdered Greenbank. Of course, with these latest deaths and the likely 'Fourth Mafia' connection, it was looking less likely that there was an English dimension to the murders. Besides, I thought to myself, as far as the deaths of Bellomo and Calabrese were concerned, presumably Helen had been in the same bed as Matthew White at the time of their deaths and so could provide a convincing alibi. This was an uncomfortable thought and I did my best to shake it from my head. Seeing me shake my head, Virgilio queried what I was thinking and I came up with an

explanation – leaving out mention of Helen or her choice of
bedfellow.

'Assuming that the three murders are all connected, it's
looking more and more likely that the perpetrator was Italian,
almost certainly sent here by some very unpleasant people in
Puglia to kill the three plotters. Goodness knows how Greenbank
managed to find out what was going on, but it looks as though he
must have done, and he was murdered to silence him. As a result,
I think it's safe to say that it's looking less and less likely that he
was on the heels of somebody British. I suppose we still have to
interview the Brits here this morning and a couple of the other
English-speakers who struck us as potentially questionable, just
in case, but I have a strong feeling that what you call the Fourth
Mafia is likely to be behind everything. The bad news is that,
with the back-door camera out of order, it's now clear that we
aren't going to get any hard evidence to show who the perpetrator might be. I don't like to be pessimistic, but it's not looking
good, is it?'

'You never know, one of the other bodyguards might give us a
breakthrough. We need to question them now.' Marco was once
again trying to sound a note of optimism, but from the expressions on the faces of the others, they weren't buying it any more
than I was.

And we were right to be pessimistic. Both of the other bodyguards, Giuseppe Fosca from Naples and Arturo Torchio from
Rome, were as tight-lipped as Rossini and told the same story,
starting with Fosca. After dinner, he said they had gone with
their employers for a nightcap outside on the terrace, which had
deteriorated into a binge. It had been well past two before they
had headed up to bed and, no, he hadn't gone for a walk in the
vines in a pair of shoes with a distinctive ribbed pattern. Virgilio
pressed Fosca about his previous conviction for possession of a

weapon but the reply was a shrug of the shoulders and a mumbled answer that he'd been looking after the pistol for a friend. As for now, no, of course he hadn't brought a weapon. What sort of man did the *commissario* think he was? None of us bothered to answer that one.

Arturo Torchio was younger than the other two bodyguards, maybe in his mid-thirties, and he looked fit. When asked about his conviction for grievous bodily harm five years earlier, he replied that he'd been younger then and, anyway, the other guy 'had been asking for it'. Of the three, I felt that he was the one with most hidden menace and I found myself studying the soles of his trainers as he lounged back on his bed. Alas, the star pattern on them was a million miles from the ribbed pattern of the shoe prints I'd noticed in the vineyard. Virgilio asked him what had taken him from his native Puglia to the capital and he claimed it had been for a job opportunity, working in a Roman gym. From his broad shoulders and broken nose, I wondered whether the gym in question had specialised in boxing.

The net result was that we were back in the corridor by ten-fifteen with little or nothing to show for our early morning's work. Our frustration was palpable and Oscar must have sensed it as he did the round of all the others, sniffing their hands and nudging their legs in a show of canine solidarity. He did, at least, manage to restore a few smiles to their faces, but the stubborn silence of our interviewees was discouraging. One thing upon which we were all in agreement was that, unless a very clever assassin had crept in from outside, one or more of the men we'd just interviewed was in all likelihood a murderer. Personally, I tended to discount Salvatore Rossini, Cassano's minder, but I couldn't really give a reason for this apart from just a good old-fashioned copper's hunch. The other three men, on the other hand, could easily have done it. Either Cassano had deliberately eliminated his two partners, for financial or other reasons, or one or both of the other two bodyguards had come with instructions to kill.

Virgilio glanced at his watch. 'We're supposed to be interviewing the British guests from ten-thirty, so why don't we head down to the bar and get ourselves a coffee before that?'

We ordered our coffees and went out onto the terrace. As the sergeant had said, an engineer was on a stepladder doing his best to fix the broken CCTV camera, and I reflected how different things would have been for us if it had been operating last night or on Tuesday afternoon. We sat down and admired the scenic view over the vineyard. Over to one side was the swimming pool surrounded by sun loungers and umbrellas, with a number of people already splashing about in the water. Straight in front of us were the regular rows of the vines and, as I had thought, it was less than a hundred yards from here to the scenes of the two recent murders, where figures in overalls and masks were trawling for evidence.

I saw the waiter talking to the engineer and when he brought us our coffees, he passed on what he'd just been told. 'The engineer says that the camera wasn't broken, it was sabotaged. One of the wires had been pulled out. He says there's no way it could have been accidental. This was done deliberately.'

By the murderer.

12

THURSDAY MORNING

The interviews with the Brits and the other English speakers who had struck us a suspicious the previous day took place in the same library room as before. The Swedish man, Nils Andersson, was still looking nervous and it took me a bit of time to find out what was worrying him. He finally confessed that on Tuesday afternoon, he hadn't been in his room having a siesta on his own, but in a different room and bed belonging to a fellow Swede, Olga Berg, currently working here on the front desk. His nervousness came from the fact that he had a wife back in Stockholm. Virgilio had a few strong words to say to him about the inadvisability of lying during a murder investigation and Andersson left the room looking chastened. Olga Berg was then summoned and she confirmed his story, although she begged us not to tell the manager. In fact, this very neatly gave both of them an alibi for the murder of Anthony Greenbank and we agreed that they were both in the clear.

The next interviewee was a large American – and he looked about seven feet tall – who had struck me as suspicious. He turned out to be a famous basketball player in his own country and the nervousness when he'd been questioned the previous day was explained by the fact that he'd been trying to stay out of the limelight. Apparently, his coach had allowed him a week off to rest a tweaked hamstring, but hadn't given him permission to leave New York, let alone travel to Europe. If it came out that he'd been taking an illicit holiday in Tuscany, he would be in big trouble. As with Nils Andersson, we agreed that this story rang true and tended to remove him from the suspicious list.

We quickly worked our way through the Brits, checking to see whether any of them might have occupied a position that would have allowed them to commit fraud on a sufficiently grand scale for an investigative journalist to be interested in them. There were nine of them, of which three were couples well into their seventies, and so unlikely to have been up to strangling Greenbank or cracking the skulls of the two dodgy Italians. None of these were still working and none had a suspicious background. This left us with three people – a forty-four-year-old writer from Hampshire travelling on his own, Matthew White and Helen. Virgilio chose to interview the writer first.

His name was Vincent Ogilvie and he claimed to be a successful author of international crime thrillers, writing under the pen name V. C. Jonas. I vaguely remembered reading one of his books some time ago. This had been recommended to me by my daughter, who had read a lot of his stuff. He told us he was over here in Italy to do research and when I queried the nature of this, our ears pricked up.

'I'm interested in the Mafia. You may think it strange that I'm here and not down south or in Sicily, but I've heard that a lot of Mafia money's being laundered in other parts of Italy and beyond – including London – and apparently, Tuscany has seen a lot of this recently.' He looked across at me and winked. 'Maybe you could ask the *commissario* or the inspector if they have any experience of this sort of thing. It would be fascinating and very useful for my research.'

I passed on the message automatically, but my brain was whirring. It certainly sounded like quite a coincidence that this man was here on the trail of people doing exactly what Cassano and his two companions had come here to do. However, I failed to see what possible reason Ogilvie could have had to commit a double or even triple murder, but he was tall and strongly built and he looked as though he would have been capable. Could he really be our killer?

Virgilio's answer didn't help the writer's research. 'Please tell Mr Ogilvie that what he's telling us is not news to me, but I'm not at liberty to reveal any detail of specific cases. Could you ask him why he chose to come to this particular hotel?'

I relayed the message and he just shrugged. 'I always use the same online booking site and this hotel looked good. I'm very impressed with the place, and the fact that they've even arranged a few murders for me is over and above what I was expecting.' He gave us a decidedly cheeky grin. 'Please tell the *commissario* I promise not to put him in my next book, but I will draw on the experience of being interviewed by the Italian police – and it's been very professionally done, if you don't mind me saying so. Tell me, what role does the dog play? Is he a sniffer dog?'

Sensing that he was being talked about, Oscar opened one eye and stretched as I answered on his behalf. 'He's a sniffer all right, but I'm not at liberty to tell you his exact job description.'

'If you like, I'll slip him into my next book. What's his name?'

'His name's Fido.' There was no way I was going to let fame go to Oscar's head.

When Ogilvie had left the room, the four of us discussed what we'd heard, agreeing that it was a remarkable coincidence that he had an interest in exactly the sort of people who had ended up dead, but Marco summed it up succinctly.

'But there's surely no earthly reason why he would want to kill these three people.'

The sergeant nodded in agreement. 'He's a writer, not a killer.'

Virgilio gave me a quizzical look and I responded. 'I tend to agree with the sergeant. Still, anything's possible but, like you, I also doubt that he's a murderer.'

He dropped his pen and looked around at the three of us. 'I agree.' He glanced at the list on the desk in front of him. 'That leaves us with just two more suspects – well, only one real suspect as I think we can safely say that Dan's ex is in the clear.'

Before I could comment, his phone rang and we saw him listening intently. At that moment, my own phone beeped and I saw that it was a message from my journalist friend, Jess Barnes.

> Hi Dan. Not a lot I can tell you about Greenbank except that he was definitely on the up, with a number of high-profile scoops revealing wrongdoings by big multinational companies. I should imagine there's no shortage of people delighted to see him dead. A friend of a friend at the Express says she thinks his latest investigation might have involved Italy, but she said he was always very secretive. Sorry I can't give you more. Hope it helps. Jess x

I had time to send her a quick thank you before Virgilio's call ended and he set down his phone. 'Well, that was interesting. Gianni will send photos of the casts of the shoeprints found in the vineyard, but the most interesting thing is that initial results of blood tests on Bellomo show that he'd been drugged before being murdered and it could well be that the same will turn out to be the case for Calabrese as well. Anybody want to hazard a guess what drug was used?' He didn't give us time to reply. 'Fluni-trazepam – sound familiar?'

He looked around at us with a little smile. Marco and Dini shook their heads and, although I did know that this was better known as Rohypnol, the date rape drug, I said nothing. No point in showing up the two very efficient officers.

Virgilio was positively beaming by this time. 'Also known as Rohypnol and we all know what that's used for. Easily slipped into a drink and undetectable – especially if the drinker was already seriously drunk. I reckon our killer drugged Calabrese and Bellomo, led them into the vines one by one and killed them.'

This was very interesting. 'So that explains how the killer or killers were able to get the men into the vines. With Rohypnol, the victim becomes acquiescent and easy to manipulate.'

Marco joined in excitedly. 'Then it has to be one or more of the bodyguards, surely.'

Virgilio was thinking along the same lines. 'It certainly seems that way, although I'm not ruling out a professional hitman sent from Puglia. Now, a question for the three of you before we inter-view Mr White: do we think the murder of the first victim, Anthony Greenbank, is connected with these latest deaths?'

Marco and Dini nodded immediately and, although I tended to agree with them, I sounded a note of caution. 'That's how it looks, although I'm still puzzled how a British journalist could have found out about this highly secret meeting.'

Virgilio nodded. 'I know what you mean, but so much points towards the cases being linked. What we need to do is to find some proof. Dini, as soon as the photos of the shoeprints arrive, circulate them and organise a fingertip search of the rooms belonging to the three bodyguards and Cassano. In the mean-time, we'll interview Mr White and, unless he breaks down and confesses, I see no reason to keep him or your ex-wife, Dan, here any longer. I understand they intend to fly home tonight.'

Matthew White came in looking as cocky as before and I felt myself bristle but, of course, the fact that he'd been sleeping with Helen wasn't going to endear him to me, and I struggled to keep a neutral expression on my face when I asked the questions.

'The *commissario* has called you back in because we've discovered that the first victim was a journalist, specialising in fraud investigations. We feel that there might be a British connection here so please could you tell us more about your background, your business and, in particular, the unfortunate food-poisoning incidents a couple of years ago.'

He jumped as if he'd been pinched and I scrutinised him carefully while he answered. Along with annoyance, I felt I spotted something else – maybe even guilt? 'That's ancient history. I bought some sausage that was off, some people got sick, but nobody died. End of story.' He began to look and sound belligerent. 'The police weren't involved, just one tabloid journalist, and it all blew over. There's no more to it than that.'

Virgilio allowed a more conciliatory note to enter his voice. 'There's no need to feel aggrieved, Mr White. We're investigating a triple murder and I'm sure you can understand that we have to ask difficult questions. Now, what about your business? You told us you were a restaurateur. How's that going?'

White started to look a bit less irritated and sound more bullish. 'It's going well. I own a chain of restaurants in London.'

Remembering what Tricia had told me, I couldn't resist putting him on the spot. 'Two of them recently closed, I believe. Was that to do with the food-poisoning scandal? That can't have helped your cash flow.'

He shot me a dirty look, and a far from professional surge of satisfaction went through me. 'I closed two so as to concentrate on the other more profitable ones and, no, I'm not short of money.' He waved a hand. 'I wouldn't be staying here if I had money worries. I doubt very much whether you police officers could afford to stay in a place like this.'

I very nearly repeated what Helen had told me about these few days being a freebie, but I didn't want to drop her in it, so I said nothing to him and just translated his words to the others. Virgilio, in spite of what he says, speaks pretty good English and he must have already understood the taunt, but nothing showed on his face as he continued the questions.

'And is this trip for business or pleasure?'

'A bit of both. I'm here to source food and wine for my restaurants, but it's good to get a few days off.'

As agreed with Virgilio and Marco, I did a little bit of digging. 'So is that why you went down to the winery on Tuesday afternoon?'

'Tuesday... I didn't... I spent the afternoon at...' He was suddenly looking less sure of himself, so I piled on the pressure.

'At the pool, yes, I know that's what you told us but it's not true, is it, Mr White? You were seen on CCTV heading for the winery after lunch.' I was taking a chance, but time wasn't on our side as he would be leaving for the airport later today.

There was silence for a few moments before his shoulders slumped and he dropped his eyes.

'I'm sorry, I forgot.' I felt sure that even Oscar could hear the insincerity in his voice. White must have heard it himself as he hastened to add an explanation. 'I didn't go anywhere near the winery, but I did get up and go into the vineyard for a walk...' He corrected himself again. 'If you must know, I had to make a personal phone call and I didn't want my current companion to overhear.'

The offhand way he referred to Helen, using the word 'current,' didn't bode well for the longevity of the relationship, but I made no comment. When all was said and done, my ex-wife's love life wasn't my business. 'How long were you away? Can the person you called confirm that's what happened?'

'Yes, of course. As for how long, I suppose I was away for half an hour, maybe three quarters.'

Long enough to commit murder.

I asked him to provide the phone number and we noted it down. After that, we questioned White further and he told us he'd been with Helen all last night, but I resolved to check that with her. We all tried firing questions at him but without getting any more out of him. Finally, Virgilio gave him a serious reprimand for lying to the police and sent him out. After the door had closed, he looked across at the three of us. 'There's one thing in his favour: the fact that he bought the CCTV story makes it less likely that he was involved with the murders. The camera by the back door has been out of action since Tuesday morning and if he was the person who sabotaged that, he would have known we were lying.'

Marco nodded in agreement. 'But the fact remains that he has no alibi for as much as forty-five minutes on Tuesday afternoon. He could easily be Greenbank's killer, but why? What do you think, Dan?'

'You're right, he had opportunity, he looks strong enough to strangle somebody, so he had means, but unless we can come up with a motive, I can't see how you can possibly arrest him and charge him.' I pulled out my phone. 'Shall I try phoning that number he gave us? I'd be interested to see who's at the other end. Of course, even if the person who answers confirms that he called, that doesn't prove anything. He could easily have made the call while he was walking down to the winery, but it's worth a go.'

I dialled the number. It was a UK number and the voice that answered me was unmistakably English, quite possibly from the East End of London, an area where I had spent my early years in the force.

'Hello, who's that?' It was a woman's voice.

'Hello, I'm phoning on behalf of the Italian police. There's been a murder and we're investigating everybody who was nearby when it happened. Could you tell us please if you know a man called Matthew White?'

'Matt, of course I know him. We've been living together for three years. He's not involved, is he?'

A wave of anger pulsed through me, which had nothing to do with the case, but I took a deep breath and carried on. 'Are you aware that he's currently in Tuscany?'

'Yes, he told me; restaurant business is what he said.'

'Have you spoken to him recently?'

'Only briefly a couple of days ago. He called me on Tuesday afternoon, but it was a very quick call, barely a minute or two, just to ask how my appointment with the midwife went. I'm due next month.'

Thirty years in the murder squad had inevitably brought me into contact with some of the baser elements of the population, and Matthew White certainly fell into that category. How on earth had Helen managed to get herself involved with a rat like this and, more to the point, was it my duty to tell her the truth about him – and what was the full truth? He was certainly a low life, but was he a murderer as well?

13

THURSDAY MORNING

When the call ended, I gave the police officers a summary of what the woman had told me and read disbelief on their faces. The sergeant was the first to react.

'What a swine! What an appalling way to treat two women!'

Marco joined in with some colourful swear words – the Tuscans have some excellent insults in their vocabulary – but we all knew that we needed to make a decision as to what should happen to Mr White. Virgilio put it into words.

'The fact that he has the moral fibre of a slug doesn't help us pin any one of these murders on him. The fact is that we're still very short of hard evidence against anybody.'

'And he's due to leave this afternoon, maybe sooner.' Marco looked across at the sergeant. 'Call in his companion. Maybe she can give us a bit more information.' As she got up, he glanced at me. 'Do we tell your ex-wife about White's pregnant lady friend?'

I had been asking myself the same question and I shook my head. Satisfying as it would be to make Helen fully aware of what kind of rat she was with, it would only hurt her even more, and I didn't want to do that. 'Personally, I don't see the point. Let's just ask her if she has anything to add to what she said yesterday.' I saw Virgilio nodding in agreement.

Helen came in looking weary but she managed a little smile when she saw me. Oscar immediately got to his feet and padded across to station himself beside her as she sat down.

Marco started the questions this time and, as usual, I translated. 'With regard to the man murdered on Tuesday, we now know that he was an investigative journalist. Can you think of any reason why he might have been interested in you or your companion?'

She shook her head uncertainly so I added a few words of encouragement. 'You'll be interested to hear that White's changed his story and told us he wasn't beside you at the pool all afternoon on Tuesday. He volunteered that information and we didn't mention that you'd told me about your doubts.' An expression of relief appeared on her face and I continued. 'He said he went for a walk in the vines, but he could have gone down to the winery. Can you think of any reason why the journalist might have been interested in him?'

She didn't reply immediately, clearly thinking hard. 'Not really. I'm pretty sure he's been having financial troubles, but I can't see why that would make him a person of interest to a journalist.'

Virgilio cut in, speaking pretty reasonable English. 'What about his friends back in the UK or here? Any with whom you felt uncomfortable?'

She shook her head. 'I don't know any of his friends and I've never even been to one of his restaurants.' Her expression turned to one of embarrassment and she appeared to be addressing herself to the sergeant rather than to me or the other men. 'To be perfectly honest, this has all been a huge mistake. I barely know the man and I still can't understand what made me say yes to his invitation to come to Tuscany with him. He seemed nice but, like I say, I know so little about him. I'm sorry.'

She looked so downcast, I almost felt like getting up and going over to give her a hug, but I stayed rooted to my seat while Marco continued. 'I believe you're flying back to the UK today. What time are you planning on leaving the hotel?'

'Our flight leaves Florence just before seven so we're going to have lunch here and then leave around four or four-thirty. We've already vacated our room.'

I glanced at my watch and saw that it was a quarter to twelve. Meanwhile, Marco had almost finished the questions. 'You may already have heard, but there were two more murders here at the hotel overnight. Please can you confirm where you and your companion were last night between ten and, say, three?'

'We were together. We were late in to dinner and it was ten-thirty before we finished. From there, we went back to the room and Matthew was with me all night.' Her cheeks flushed and she avoided meeting my eye.

Marco pressed her a bit harder. 'Presumably, you went to sleep at some point.'

Her blushes deepened.

'So how can you be sure that he didn't leave the room?'

'You're right, I can't be 100 per cent sure. To be honest, we shared a bottle of wine over dinner and that always makes me sleepy, but I'm pretty certain he didn't go out.'

This appeared to provide a reasonable but not watertight alibi for the recent killings, but a shadow still hung over White with regard to Tuesday afternoon.

After a few more questions and answers, Marco dismissed her and she shot me another little smile before leaving, but she said nothing and we didn't even shake hands this time. As the door closed behind her, I couldn't repress a feeling of relief.

The sergeant picked up her phone. 'The pathologist has sent over the photo of the shoeprints found beside the two most recent victims. I'll go and organise a search of the rooms now.'

Marco nodded at her and headed for the door. 'I need a bit of fresh air, so I'm going to take a walk.'

After the others had left, Virgilio stretched and looked across at me. 'What about lunch, Dan? Do you have plans? The least I can do is to buy you a good meal.'

'Thanks for the offer but I'm taking Anna out for lunch. We're going back to the place you took us to yesterday. I would ask you to join us, but it's her birthday and she's expecting an intimate meal with just the two of us. You know how it is.'

He grinned. 'But at least you remembered it was her birthday. That's more than I did last year and I'm still in the doghouse with Lina as a result.'

I grinned back. 'I have to confess that I almost forgot, so I need this lunch to go really well.'

He wished me luck and I went out to give Oscar a little walk before Anna arrived. We did a quick ten-minute circuit in the vines before heading back to the hotel. It was still blisteringly hot and I got the feeling even Oscar was quite happy to make it a short walk. To my surprise, when I got to the front steps, Helen appeared out of the glass door, glancing nervously over her shoulder.

'Dan, I've been hoping I'd catch you. I just wanted to say thank you. I don't know what I would have done without your support.'

'I didn't do very much but I'm glad if it helped. Can I ask you something?' She nodded so I continued. 'Did you mean what you said about ending things between you and Matthew White?' She nodded again. 'I'm pleased to hear it. We've been learning more about him and none of it's to his credit. You can do a lot better than somebody like him, believe me.'

'I do believe you, and I feel such a fool.' She caught my eye, the expression on her face one of embarrassment and contrition 'I'm a fifty-four-year-old woman and I should have known better than to behave like a silly teenager. It all sounded so romantic – the luxury hotel, the Tuscan hills – but the reality was anything but romantic. I've been an idiot, Dan.'

I gave her a little smile. This was a very different Helen from the bitter, vindictive woman who had divorced me. Maybe the divorce had been positive for both of us. 'We all do foolish things, Helen. Don't beat yourself up. Do me a favour, will you? Send me a text message when you get back home tonight so I know you're safe.'

'Oh, Dan!' She reached up and put her arms around my shoulders so she could kiss me. Instinctively, I turned my head so that the kiss landed on my cheek. She kissed me once again and then to my relief, stepped back. 'You can be such a sweetie sometimes. I'd better go. I have to meet Matt in the dining room. Thanks again and look after yourself.' She bent down to pet Oscar before turning on her heel and disappearing back inside again. As she did so, I heard footsteps behind me and a voice at my ear.

'Do all your suspects treat you like that, Dan?' Anna was doing her best to sound casual but I knew her well enough by now to catch the suspicion in her voice. I whirled around and caught hold of both her hands while Oscar stood up on his hind legs to greet her.

'*Ciao, bella*, I'm so pleased to see you. Happy birthday! Oscar, get off, you'll make a mess of her dress.' I didn't recognise the light-blue silk dress so I took a chance. 'You look lovely, Anna. Is that a new dress?'

She produced a little smile, but it was the sort of smile a mother gives a child who's dropped his ice cream on the floor. 'It was new before you and I went to the faculty Christmas party, but thanks for the compliment anyway.'

I looked around. 'Where's your car?' She pointed so I indicated my van. 'Shall we leave yours here and go in the van? It's only ten minutes away.'

'Fine by me, but don't I get a look at the inside of this hotel first? It does look very swish. Or are you afraid I'll meet even more women in there who fling their arms around you and kiss you?' The smile was still there but it was wearing thin.

I knew I had no choice. 'Of course, come on in and I'll show you around.'

Oscar and I led her inside and I showed her the sumptuous lounges, introduced her to Sergeant Dini, took her out to view the terrace and pool and finally stuck our heads into the restaurant. To my surprise, there was no sign of Helen or her man, and I breathed a sigh of relief, but this turned out to be premature. As we were turning to leave, who should appear but the two of them. White brushed past us without acknowledging my presence, but Helen and Anna exchanged glances that it didn't take Hercule Poirot to interpret. No words were spoken and I hastily led Anna out into the corridor, sweat beading on my back in spite of the efficient air con in here. As we walked back along the corridor to the lobby in silence, I caught a glance from Oscar and it looked as though he rolled his eyes. I had a feeling he realised that I'd dug myself into a hole. *I* certainly did.

Without a word being spoken, we crossed the car park and climbed into the van. Fortunately, it had been protected from direct sunlight by a pair of enormous umbrella pines and the temperature inside was bearable. Even so, I opened all the windows and savoured the breeze as we coasted down the drive towards the entrance.

Finally managing to pull myself together, I drew up in the shade of a pair of cypress trees and stopped the engine. I turned towards Anna and, as I did so, I spotted a big, hairy, black face eyeing me over the top of the back seat. Drawing confidence from his presence, I launched into the explanation I'd been planning.

'There's something I've been meaning to tell you since yesterday. My intention was to wait until we had a lovely meal and then break the news to you at the end, but I think it's best we talk about it now. You see, that woman back at the hotel is my ex-wife.'

An expression of surprise flooded Anna's face. 'Your ex-wife is here? What's going on, and who was that man she was with? I didn't like the look of him.'

'I had no idea she'd found herself another man or that they were going to be here in Italy until Virgilio, Marco and I found ourselves interviewing her yesterday morning. I'm sure you can imagine how much of a shock it was for me when she walked in. She answered the questions and then left the room, and as far as I was concerned, that was the last I was going to see of her until I got called back in this morning because there have been two more deaths.'

The surprised expression was still on her face. 'Two more murders?'

I nodded. 'That makes three in three days. Anyway, as a result, we've had to interview a load of people again and because, just like you, we didn't like the look of her boyfriend either, we had to call him and her back in for more questions. She told us she didn't trust him and that she was going to dump him as soon as they get back to England tonight. What you saw outside on the steps was her saying thank you to me for keeping her out of it and, in answer to your original question, no, murder suspects don't usually kiss me on the cheeks.'

'I see.' Her expression was a bit more relaxed now but I could tell something was still bothering her. I felt pretty sure I knew what it was so I decided to tackle it head-on.

'I was going to tell you yesterday, but because we weren't meeting up in person, I didn't think it was the sort of thing to talk about on the phone. As you can imagine, the two of you bumping into each other was not part of the plan.'

There was a long pause before she replied. Finally, she looked me straight in the eye. 'Should I be worried, Dan?'

'Worried? No, of course not. Remember, this is the woman who divorced me and it's all over between us. She means nothing to me any more.' As I said it, I knew that I meant it, but Anna still looked doubtful.

'I wonder if she feels the same way about you. Forgetting for a moment about the hug and the kisses, I could tell from the way she looked at you that there was still something there. Are you quite sure I don't need to be worried?'

I caught hold of both her hands in mine and gave them a reassuring squeeze. 'Of course I'm sure. I'm with you now and she's my *ex*-wife. Apart from this most unexpected meeting, I doubt if I'll see her again for a long, long time. I promise you there's nothing between Helen and me, and there never will be again. Please believe me.'

I avoided looking at Oscar.

14

THURSDAY AFTERNOON

Lunch at the porcupine restaurant was excellent once again. This time, we both opted for a starter of bresaola along with slices of cold roast aubergine covered in soft goat's cheese, served on a bed of rocket leaves. I had no intention of repeating the disappointing Rockstar Chianti experience so we drank the house red, which was head and shoulders better. We followed the antipasti with *crespelle al tartufo*. Since settling in Tuscany, I'd developed a real taste for these savoury pancakes folded and filled with cheese. The flakes of white truffles gave a whole new dimension to the experience and I added this to my ever-expanding list of the best dishes I'd ever eaten. I glanced across at Anna as we ate. She'd been more communicative since my explanation in the van, although I could still sense some uncertainty in her and I'd been doing my best to cheer her up. For his part, Oscar had positioned himself at her side where he stared up at her in adoration throughout the meal – although this might have been cupboard love as she still sometimes falls for his 'Dan doesn't feed me, I'm starving to death' routine.

I got her to tell me how things were going in the Medieval

and Renaissance History Studies department and, in return, I gave her a brief summary of the investigation at the hotel, making sure I steered the conversation away from the subject of my ex-wife. I had just got to the point where I was going to have to admit that we still had no proof against anybody when my phone started vibrating. I could see who the caller was so I left it on the table, unwilling to answer it and spoil what was hopefully developing into an intimate afternoon. Anna caught my eye.

'Who is it?'

'Marco Innocenti. It'll be work, but this lunch is about you and me celebrating your birthday.'

'Answer it, you idiot.' She gave me a smile. 'I know you want to. Thank you for the thought, but you have your work to do just like I have.'

With a show of reluctance, I answered the phone. '*Ciao*, Marco, what's new?'

'All hell's broken out here.' He sounded breathless. 'There's been another murder, and I've arrested the killer.'

'Another murder? Who's been killed?'

'Salvatore Rossini, Davide Cassano's bodyguard.'

'How did it happen?'

'Strangulation, just like Greenbank, very recently, probably between eleven and twelve today. Two of my men found him in his room when they were searching for the shoes that left the distinctive pattern in the earth alongside this morning's two bodies. He was lying face down on his bed. Signs of a struggle but no immediate clues. Forensics have just turned up now and they'll start going through everything.'

'If there's no evidence, how come you've identified and arrested the killer? Who is it?'

'Matthew White, your ex-wife's man. He and she checked out at noon with their bags, but our people found a pair of shoes matching the pattern of the casts stuffed in the waste bin. He's upstairs under guard and I'm hoping you'll be able to come back and translate for me while I question him.'

'Wow! So do you think he's responsible for all four murders?'

'It certainly looks that way.'

'But why?' In a way, it didn't surprise me that White had been revealed as one of the bad guys, but I was at a loss to come up with a motive. 'Why kill four people?'

'We're working on the basis that he was the hitman sent to eliminate the three big fish. Presumably, he killed the journalist because he was getting too nosey. Maybe the journalist discovered White was a hired killer and that's why he followed him to Italy. White killed Bellomo and Calabrese in the small hours of this morning and then Rossini an hour ago, probably because the guy saw something out on the terrace last night that he shouldn't have seen.'

I shot a glance across the table at Anna, who looked miles away. 'What about his partner, Helen Thompson? What's happened to her?'

'Nothing. Her bag's been searched, but she's clean. As far as I'm concerned, she can leave. The impression I get is that she'll be only too happy to get away from White.'

'And what about him? Has he admitted committing the murders?'

'Very much the opposite. As far as we can understand, he's screaming his innocence and demanding that we call the British embassy to help him.'

'I suppose a confession would have been too good to be true.' But the fact was that this whole thing was sounding too good to be true. What kind of moron would leave behind the distinctive shoes he'd worn when committing a murder? And could I see a bunch of hoods from Puglia employing a hired killer all the way from the UK? The answer to that was no, but this was Marco's case and I didn't want to tread on his toes. Although it went against the grain, I congratulated him, and he repeated his request for help with the questioning. I put my hand over the microphone and looked across at Anna, who immediately revealed that she had been following my side of the conversation.

'I gather there's been another murder. Who was it?'

'One of the bodyguards we interviewed this morning.'

'And who has Marco arrested?'

So much for steering the conversation away from my ex-wife. 'A man called Matthew White. You saw him an hour ago with my ex-wife.'

Her eyes opened wide. 'I told you I didn't like the look of him, but a murderer!'

'The thing is... Marco's asking if I could go back there and help with translating when he questions White. Would you mind...?'

She reached over, gripped my free hand, and smiled at me. 'Of course I don't mind.' She sounded as if she meant it.

'But I promised to give you a lovely lunch and then the plan was to spend the rest of the day together. I can't go off and leave you.'

'You can and you must.' She sounded quite determined.

'Well, if you're sure...' I spoke to Marco again and told him I'd be there in half an hour or so.

At that moment, our main course arrived. We had both chosen the same thing: confit duck breast with a ginger sauce, accompanied by roast sweet potatoes. I devoted myself to this for five minutes or so before Anna's voice interrupted me.

'What's the matter, Dan? I would have expected you to be celebrating the success of the investigation. Surely solving a case involving four murders is a magnificent achievement.'

I took a sip of wine before answering honestly. 'There's something about this that doesn't stack up. I'm struggling to come up with a motive that would make White commit murder and the only hard evidence seems to be a pair of shoes that could easily have been planted in the man's room.'

'So what are you going to do about it?'

'It's not my case. It's being handled by Marco and it's his first big case. All right, he's had Virgilio and me holding his hand – well, interfering, really – but the last thing I want to do is to turn things upside down. I'll help him with interpreting but I can't butt in unless I'm asked.'

'I know you, Dan Armstrong. You can't let an innocent man take the rap for something he didn't do – however untrustworthy he might appear to us. When you go back to the hotel, you need to get to the bottom of it.'

'I suppose you're right, but I don't want to screw things up for Marco.'

'Try and be as diplomatic as you can. I know diplomacy isn't your forte but do your best, and if justice ends up being done, he'll understand. Just promise me if you bump into your ex-wife, you won't fall in love with her all over again.' There was a humorous note to her voice but I could hear the insecurity behind it and I reached for her hands again.

'That's all in the past. I told you and I meant it. Please don't worry about that.'

'All right, I trust you and I believe you. Now why don't you hurry up and finish your duck? Order a lemon sorbet for me and a panna cotta for you, and then you need to go back to the hotel. I'll pick up my car from there and drive back to the library for a few more hours. I've got piles of work to do and I'll see you at your place tonight. All right?'

Twenty minutes later, we were back in the van, heading for

the hotel. When we got there, Anna gave me a kiss and wished me luck before driving off. I let Oscar out of the van and both of us knew that I had something far more important to do than trying to solve four murders. Under his unwavering gaze, I pulled out his food bowl, filled it from the pack I had brought with me and set it down alongside a bowl of water for him. Within three minutes, he had hoovered the lot down and I was able to head for the main entrance with him.

The first person I saw was Sergeant Dini, standing alongside her car, so I made straight for her with Oscar bounding ahead of me. She smiled when she saw him and gave him a cuddle while I remembered Anna's words and tried hard to think of the most diplomatic way of sowing seeds of doubt about the guilt of the man they had arrested. As it turned out, I needn't have bothered with diplomacy.

'Erm, I was wondering how sure you are that Matthew White's the perpetrator. Leaving his shoes in his room strikes me as very amateurish.'

An expression of relief flooded across her face. 'Oh, thank goodness. I thought I was the only one. The *commissario*'s gone for lunch and Inspector Innocenti's convinced that White's some kind of international professional hitman. Surely if the guy's a pro, he wouldn't have done anything as stupid as leave his shoes lying around in a waste basket. Besides, he has an alibi for last night's two murders.' She caught my eye and looked a bit embarrassed. 'An alibi provided by your ex-wife. I'm sorry, but if he went off and killed Bellomo and Calabrese last night, it means she must have been lying to protect him. The impression I get from her is that she can't wait to get away from him, so I find it hard to believe she'd be prepared to perjure herself to provide him with an alibi. So, all in all, I don't think he's the murderer.'

I beamed at her. 'Sergeant Dini, you're going to go far. I'm sure you're right. So if we both agree that White isn't the killer – or at least he isn't the killer of all four men – then who is? I'm still not convinced that all four murders are linked. Of course, it seems logical to lump them all together, but I'm at a loss to come up with a compelling motive. The more I think about these three most recent murders, the more certain I am that they were carried out on the orders of a bunch of mafiosi down in Puglia and it's hardly credible that a British journalist could have somehow stumbled on this meeting of conspirators. I have a hunch that he was here for a completely different reason but, like I say, it's just a hunch.'

As I was speaking, a scene of crime officer in overalls, mask and gloves came out of the front door holding a clear plastic bag. He held it out towards Dini. 'We've just found this, Sergeant. It'll need to be analysed, but we reckon it's Rohypnol.'

Inside the bag was a little plastic bottle. It was almost empty but not quite. Lying at the bottom was a single light-green pill. Hopefully, lab analysis would confirm what we had just heard.

Dini turned the bag over in her hands, studying it carefully. 'Thanks a lot, Mantovani. Where did you find this? In White's room?'

To my surprise, he shook his head. 'No, we found it dropped in the cistern in the bathroom belonging to Arturo Torchio.'

Dini and I exchanged glances. Of the three bodyguards we'd interviewed this morning, Torchio was the one who had struck me as most potentially dangerous. This discovery put him right back in the frame.

Or did it?

I was the first to state the obvious. 'So who put it there? Was it Torchio, trying to hide the evidence, or was it White in an attempt to muddy the waters, or maybe it was the real killer who was neither of the two? Okay, Torchio's cistern is a bit less obvious than White's waste basket, but the killer must have known that you would search the rooms very carefully indeed. If Torchio really was the murderer, he would have known that Rohypnol dissolves in water. Leaving a pill in the bottle for us to find strikes me as either incredibly stupid or a deliberate attempt by somebody else to frame Torchio. Yes, this casts a shadow over the guy, but I wouldn't call it conclusive.'

The sergeant nodded slowly. 'Of course, it could be that he's incredibly stupid. In my experience, there aren't many criminal masterminds going around. But if it was put there to frame him, who did it?'

I started counting on my fingers. 'As I see it, there's Cassano, the last of the three big fish. Maybe he's behind all the murders, and they've not been done on the orders of the Puglia Mafia at all. With his two partners dead, he probably stands to pocket the seven million euros in the company's bank account and maybe become the boss of this new version of the "Fourth Mafia". Second is the remaining bodyguard, Fosca. He may have been sent to kill the conspirators. Number three is Matthew White, followed by Ogilvie, the English writer, although I'm at a loss to find a motive for him to have committed murder. Number five is the great unknown: a very clever hitman sent to eliminate the three conspirators, but who so far hasn't left a trace of his existence. Take your pick.'

I saw the sergeant digest what I had just said and then she caught my eye. 'If it really is the work of a very clever hitman – or woman – we're going to need a lot more evidence than we currently have. Managing to kill four people – three of them right under the noses of the police – is the sign of a real pro. Maybe we aren't going to solve these cases at all.'

I looked for something to say to cheer her up but, in the end, all I could do was shrug.

15

THURSDAY AFTERNOON

Dini accompanied me to the library, where a satisfied-looking Marco Innocenti was standing by the desk looking down at Matthew White on the seat in front of him. White had been handcuffed and there was a police officer on either side of him. This all seemed a bit excessive, but presumably Marco was trying to frighten White into a confession. Marco smiled as I appeared at the door.

'Thanks for coming, Dan. I think we've got our murderer.'

I glanced across at White and was pleased to see him looking less cocky than the last time we'd met. There was no sign of comprehension on his face. Presumably, when his father had adopted an English name, he had also given up on any attempt to teach his children his own native language. Still, just in case the lack of comprehension was an act, I beckoned to Marco.

'Hi, Marco, can I have a quiet word with you outside for a moment?'

He looked surprised but he didn't object. I waited until we were out in the corridor with the door closed before I voiced my doubts. 'Before we start questioning White, has it occurred to you that this guy has an alibi for last night provided by my ex-wife? I definitely think she was telling the truth and I see no reason why she should lie to protect him. In fact, I get the impression she's just dying to get away from him.' Silently repeating the word 'diplomacy' to myself, I added a few more words. 'Of course, she could be lying, but that would mean she's involved in this, and I really can't believe it of her.'

I've always thought that Marco was a good detective and I was pleased to discover that he had already considered this. 'I can't believe it either, but what if she was asleep when he slipped out to commit the murders?' Before I could voice my doubts – back when we'd been married, Helen's lynx-like hearing had meant that just about every time I'd rolled over in bed, I had woken her – he explained his rationale.

'Rohypnol, Dan. White had already successfully drugged at least two people outside on the terrace – more probably four if we include their bodyguards – so it would have been quite easy for him to drug her as well. A simple blood test should soon prove that one way or the other.'

I nodded slowly as the idea registered with me. 'You could well be right, Marco, but the other thing that's worrying me is the fact that he left the shoes behind in his room, and in such an obvious place as well. If he's a professional killer, clever enough to drug people, strangle people and beat two others to death, do we really think he would be that stupid? I must admit the more I think about it, the more I tend to think it's a set-up.'

Sergeant Dini held out the evidence bag containing the pill bottle. 'Forensics have just found this hidden in Arturo Torchio's bathroom. They reckon the pill is Rohypnol.'

I heard Marco snort in frustration. 'So now do we think that *Torchio* is the murderer? If he did it, then leaving this lying around was a crazy thing for him to do. Why didn't he just flush

the Rohypnol down the toilet? I think you're right and somebody's trying to frame him. And my money's still on Matthew
White.'

It was on the tip of my tongue to point out that Torchio could
just as easily have been trying to frame White by dumping his
own shoes in White's waste basket but I could see that the new
inspector had made his mind up so I stayed quiet. Along with
Sergeant Dini, I followed Marco back into the library and took a
seat beside him as he started questioning White. At first, the man
was reluctant to reply, sticking to his demand for the British
embassy in Rome to be contacted, until I spelled it out for him.

'You can contact the embassy by all means, but all that's going
to do is prolong things. If you're innocent, surely you want to get
this over and done with, don't you? Why not just answer the
inspector's questions as honestly as you can and, you never know,
you might be on a plane home to England tonight.'

I saw this register with him, so I tried Marco's first questions
again. 'Are you aware that four people have died in the last three
days, three of them in the past few hours? We now have evidence
that points to your involvement with the murders. Have you
anything to say?'

'I'm innocent; I haven't murdered anybody. I wouldn't do
anything like that.' Any last vestiges of cockiness had disappeared and I got the feeling that the severity of the situation in
which White now found himself had finally registered. Being
handcuffed can have that effect on people. 'What sort of evidence
can you possibly have against me? I haven't done anything
wrong.'

Marco didn't answer his question but fired out another of his
own. 'Where were you this morning between eleven and twelve-
thirty?'

'Me... this morning, I was interviewed yet again by you lot

and then I was out on the terrace while you interviewed my partner. When she emerged, we had a drink together and then we went for lunch.' He pointed at me. 'And *you* saw me in the dining room, didn't you?'

After rattling off a translation to the others, I confirmed to them that I had indeed seen White at around twelve-fifteen. Of course, he could still have slipped away before that to murder Rossini and plant the incriminating evidence in Torchio's room, but a thought occurred to me and I caught Marco's eye. 'Presumably the CCTV on the terrace is working again, so we should be able to check this guy's story.'

He nodded and glanced at one of the constables flanking the suspect. 'Alfieri, go to Reception and ask to see the footage from the terrace camera this morning. Hopefully, the woman who knows how it works will be there this time.' Returning his attention to White, he handed him an evidence bag containing a grey and white trainer. 'Tell me, Mr White, do you recognise this shoe?'

White looked genuinely puzzled for a few moments as he handled the clear plastic bag and studied its contents. If it was playacting, it was convincing.

'It's a shoe. Is it supposed to mean something?' He sounded as bewildered as he looked.

'It's your shoe, Mr White.'

White's expression turned to one of disgust. 'It most certainly isn't. I'd never dream of wearing anything like that. It's gross.'

'Then if it isn't your shoe, how come we found it and its companion in your hotel bedroom?'

'I have no idea, but I can assure you that it's not mine.'

'What size shoes do you take?'

'Um, ten or ten and a half.'

Marco looked puzzled so I explained. 'I wear size ten and a

half and that translates as Italian size forty-four or forty-five normally, I think.'

Marco informed us that the shoes found in White's waste bin were a size forty-five so they could have been his, although his denials sounded pretty genuine to me.

Marco carried on with his questions and I translated as before.

'Let's talk about Tuesday afternoon. We've already established that you lied when you told us you stayed by the pool all afternoon, only to change your story later. In the second version, you told us you went for a walk in the vines because you wanted to make a phone call. You were away for almost forty-five minutes, but we spoke to your partner in England and she told us that the call lasted barely a minute or two. Bearing in mind the serious position in which you now find yourself, I'm going to ask you if there's a third version – hopefully the truth this time. Tell us exactly what happened on Tuesday afternoon. It's in your best interests to give us an honest answer.'

We had to wait almost half a minute before White answered, resignation in his voice. 'All right, there *is* a third version and I promise you it's the truth this time. The reason I didn't say anything before is because I was frightened. I saw something down at the winery and I was afraid you would blame it on me.'

'What did you see, Mr White?' I found myself leaning forward and saw the other officers following every word White spoke with acute interest. Was this about to be an admission of guilt?

White cleared his throat. 'It was about half past two, and I think I might have seen a murder being committed.'

'You think you might have seen something? You don't sound very sure. Tell us what you think you saw and remember that we need complete honesty this time.'

'I went down the track to the winery because I wanted to speak to Mancini, the manager. I import a lot of their Rockstar Chianti into the UK and I wanted to discuss a big order that's due in the UK in good time for the pre-Christmas rush.' He paused and wiped both his handcuffed hands across his forehead. In spite of the air con in here, he was sweating profusely. He was clearly nervous, but did this also imply guilt?

'And did you see him?'

'No, I didn't get that far. I saw something I shouldn't have seen so I turned tail and ran back as fast as I could because I was afraid.'

'Afraid of what, Mr White?'

'I was afraid I was going to be killed.'

'Because of something you'd seen? I'll ask you again: what did you see?'

White took a deep breath and leant forward. 'When I got quite close to the winery, through the leaves of the vines, I could see a big truck pulled up alongside the cantina, the place where the wine's made and stored.'

This was potentially significant and I jumped in with a question of my own. 'What sort of truck? Can you describe it?'

White looked up at me in surprise and took a moment before answering. 'Nothing special, just a big truck, a tanker, one of those fuel-delivery lorries.'

'Can you remember any writing on it? A company name?'

He shook his head and Marco drew him back to his story. 'Carry on with your account of what you saw. A big truck, and what else?'

'About twenty metres behind the truck, I suddenly saw a figure appear from the vines with his phone in his hand, walking suspiciously slowly and quite clearly taking photos or shooting video of the scene. I could see he was uneasy as he kept glancing around nervously so I shrank back into the vines. And then, just a few seconds later, a huge great dog appeared and started snarling and barking. The man with the phone turned to run but, as he did so, another man emerged from the cantina and ran towards him, catching him by the throat and pulling him towards the open door. As they disappeared inside, I could see the photographer struggling to breathe. His face was bright red and his arms were windmilling helplessly. Like I say, I wasn't taking any chances. I turned and ran before somebody spotted me.'

'Can you describe the man taking the photos?'

'He wasn't big and he had fair hair, very fair, blond hair.'

'And the man who grabbed him and pulled him into the cantina?'

White shook his head. 'It all happened so fast, I can't really say. He was quite a bit taller than the photographer and he had dark hair, but I really can't remember much about anything because I was already turning to run away.'

'Might it have been the winery manager or another member of staff? You did say that you knew them.' Marco asked the question that was uppermost in my mind.

'I honestly can't say.' White gave Marco and me a look of supplication. 'You've got to believe me. It all happened so quickly and I was hiding in the vines so I couldn't see it clearly through the leaves. It could have been anybody.'

I had to admit that the story had a ring of truth to it, but Marco wasn't taking anything White said at face value. 'An interesting tale, but I put it to you that the person who strangled that man was you, just like you strangled a man called Salvatore Rossini up on the second floor of this hotel a couple of hours ago. Isn't that the truth?'

'No, no, no, I only *saw* what happened down at the winery. I had nothing to do with it and I don't even know anybody called

Rossini. You've got to believe me.' White was visibly upset and almost crying now. I glanced at the sergeant and saw her give an imperceptible nod of the head. If this guy was acting, he deserved an Oscar. Interestingly, there was a movement at my feet as my own Oscar stood up and padded over to sit down beside White and rest a big paw on his knee in solidarity. This, as much as White's performance, convinced me and I felt sure the man had been telling the truth this time. Not only would Oscar do a good job of judging beauty pageants, I reckon he could also do a pretty good job as a judge in a court of law – and he wouldn't need to wear a wig.

Marco carried on with the questions, pressing White on his movements last night and again before lunch today, but without any result. In the end, Marco stood up, and the sergeant and I followed him out of the room, along the corridor and into the fresh air, leaving White in the custody of the constables. As we emerged through the glass door, I spotted Virgilio's black car coming up the drive. We walked across to meet up with him.

'What are you doing back here, Dan?' He fended off Oscar's greeting affectionately. 'It's Anna's birthday; shouldn't you be with her?'

I saw Marco do a double take. 'Anna's birthday? I'm sorry, Dan, I didn't know. I shouldn't have called you back here. You should have said something.'

'That's all right, Marco, I was glad to be here to hear what White had to say. The thing is, Virgilio, we've been interviewing Matthew White again and this time, I'm pretty sure he's finally told us the truth about what happened on Tuesday afternoon. Don't you agree, Marco, Sergeant Dini?' They both nodded and I checked one detail with them. 'What about his description of the victim? Was Greenbank a small guy with blond hair?' Sergeant Dini replied with a nod and I continued. 'Assuming that nobody from up here saw the victim, this means that White is either the killer or he was telling us the truth about seeing the man being murdered.'

Virgilio looked animated and I let Marco explain the events of the last couple of hours to him, finishing with what White had told us. Virgilio listened attentively before finally turning to me. 'Dan, do you think White's the killer or not?'

I shook my head. 'Anything's possible but no, I don't. I don't like the guy and I certainly wouldn't buy a plate of salami from him, but I believed what he said in there this time. I don't think he's the killer type.'

Virgilio nodded a couple of times. 'So, if *he* isn't the murderer, then who is?'

Marco wasn't giving up. 'I still think he might be our man but I also agree that all the evidence we have against him so far is a pair of shoes discarded in plain sight. They may not even be his and the case would almost certainly be thrown out by the public prosecutor before it got to court. We need something more definite and, at the moment, we have nothing.'

Virgilio took a few moments before responding. 'Right, this is what we're going to do. I'm going to go down to the winery and interview everybody there, particularly the manager, Fabiano Mancini. About five minutes ago, I took a call from Florida Froot, telling me that her boyfriend's back from his latest wine-buying trip and is ready to be interviewed. He has an Italian name, so I assume he speaks Italian. Marco, why don't you and Dini go and interview him? Dan, if you feel like giving Oscar a walk, would you like to come down to the winery with me? Let's see if anybody down there reacts when we tell them White's story about the journalist being strangled.'

16

THURSDAY AFTERNOON

The walk down to the winery through the vineyard was very pleasant and Oscar certainly enjoyed the exercise, chasing non-existent squirrels and retrieving sticks. This afternoon, grey clouds were beginning to roll in at long last and the temperature had dropped a bit, although it was increasingly humid. It looked as though the long-awaited rain was finally on its way. I felt sure that all the local farmers, including my neighbour Fausto, would be greatly relieved, although for the imminent grape harvest, it was probably already too late to make much difference.

We were roughly halfway to the winery when Oscar emerged from the vines with a hefty chunk of wood in his mouth and proudly deposited it at my feet. I reached down to pick it up and throw it but stopped in my tracks.

'Virgilio, take a look at this.'

He stopped and came back to where I was staring at what was a three-foot-long piece of wooden post, roughly the diameter of a coffee cup. What was of particular interest was the fact that one end of the post was covered in what was unmistakably dried blood. It looked as though Oscar had found the murder weapon.

Virgilio pulled out his phone and made a call. Barely three minutes later, a young constable came running down the track towards us and Virgilio instructed him to take the post up to the villa and hand it over to Forensics for analysis. 'You'll find Labrador saliva on it but I want to know if there are any finger-prints or DNA.' After the officer had donned gloves and picked up the post, Virgilio glanced down at Oscar, who was still waiting for a stick to chase.

'Officer Oscar, another triumph. Dan, remind me to buy him a steak. Here...' He picked up a cypress branch from the ground and sent it flying down the track, pursued by Officer Oscar, tail wagging enthusiastically.

All the way down the track, Virgilio and I discussed the case, but time and time again, we came up against the problem of the lack of evidence – although hopefully, Oscar's discovery might hold the key, at least as far as the deaths at the hotel were concerned. As for motive, neither of us had much doubt about the deaths at the hotel being Mafia hits, but I still wasn't convinced that the death of the journalist down at the winery was necessarily connected and I told Virgilio so. Maybe our visit to the winery would produce some results, although Virgilio's people had already interviewed everybody down there without suspecting any of them of being involved.

As we drew nearer to the winery, I reflected on what Matthew White had just told us. He had claimed to have seen a big truck parked outside the cantina on Tuesday afternoon and, of course, the unfortunate journalist had been run over by a big truck. Might the trucks have been one and the same?

The aggressive mongrel came out to greet us with a volley of barking and, as before, it was closely followed by the man I now knew to be Guido Renzi. My eyes were immediately drawn to his mop of ginger hair. If White's story about a dark-haired man assaulting Greenbank was correct, it didn't look as though Renzi was our would-be strangler. Virgilio stopped, warily eyeing the mongrel, whose barking had now subsided to sinister growls, while Oscar appeared quite unmoved by all the aggression and sat down on the dusty earth and scratched his ear with his back leg, without a care in the world. As he did so, I studied the ground at his and our feet and I could see the impressions left in the dirt by numerous tyres, some clearly belonging to the company pickup and some considerably wider ones, among them presumably the truck seen by White on Tuesday. I noticed Virgilio's eyes looking in the same direction and I quizzed him.

'Do you think Forensics have compared the tread pattern of these tyres with those found on the body?'

'I certainly hope so, but I haven't heard back from them. I'll check.' He pulled out his warrant card and waved it in the direction of Renzi. 'I'm Commissario Pisano of the Florence murder squad and I'd like to have a few words with you, preferably away from that dog of yours – what is it, a wolf?'

Renzi nodded. 'Half wolf, we reckon. There are wolves around here. Whatever his father was, he makes a good guard dog. Come inside if you like. I'll leave him out here.'

He shouted a command at the dog, which, though incomprehensible to me, must have meant something to the mongrel, who sat down and looked on malevolently as the three of us plus Oscar went into the cantina. The only other winemaking establishments I had visited, like the one belonging to Fausto and his late father, were small fry in comparison to this place. In here, there were eight huge, stainless-steel vats in a row, each of them the size of my van standing on end, and the whole of the opposite wall was lined with pallets loaded with cartons of bottles, held in place by some industrial-sized kitchen wrap. A complex network of pipes led to and from the vats and there was an overpowering smell of wine. I felt sure that if I were to spend much time in here, I would end up with a hangover. Maybe this was the reason why the mongrel and Renzi appeared so morose. The good news was that the dog outside had finally shut up and the silence was most welcome.

There was nowhere to sit down so we stayed on our feet as Virgilio rattled off a series of questions, checking the man's name and address and learning that he had worked here for five years. After establishing his identity, Virgilio consulted his notebook and launched into questions related to the murders.

'You told my officers that you were working here on Tuesday afternoon but you didn't see anything. Is that still correct?'

'I told the female officer who interviewed me and I told this guy here with the black dog that I was out in the vines and didn't see anything.'

'What were you doing in the vines?'

'The *vendemmia* starts next week, so I've been getting ready – you know, cutting off old leaves and rotten grapes to make things easier when we start the harvest.'

'We've been told that there was a big truck parked here on Tuesday afternoon. Can you confirm or deny that?'

'I didn't see it, but we received a delivery of boxes on Tuesday. That's usually a big truck.' He pointed across the room to a couple of pallets piled high with flat-packed cardboard boxes.

'What about fuel? Were you expecting a tanker?'

He shook his head. 'Not that I'm aware of. Ask the boss.'

Virgilio caught my eye. Guido Renzi certainly wasn't producing any startling new information. Virgilio asked him how many other people worked here and received a fairly limited answer. 'There's Signor Mancini, Elena, Mauro and me, but all I can tell you is that I was here on Tuesday. As for the others, you'd better ask in the shop.'

'Where were you between eleven and twelve-thirty today?'

'Today? Why, what's happened today?' He looked genuine enough.

'Another murder. It appears that this is a dangerous place. Where were you?'

He shrugged. 'Same as Tuesday. I've been out in the vines, preparing them for the harvest.'

'Can anybody vouch for you?'

Renzi shook his head but, to my mind, his lack of an alibi wasn't necessarily suspicious. In my experience, murderers normally do their best to establish convincing alibis in advance so as to conceal the fact that they've committed the crime. Innocent people don't see the need. Of course, there are always exceptions.

Virgilio closed his notebook with a snap. 'I'll go and talk to your colleagues now. Thank you for your cooperation, Signor Renzi.'

The ginger-haired man didn't react. In fact, he didn't say another word as we went back outside, setting the mongrel off into another paroxysm of barking. As we went past, I saw Oscar shoot the canine equivalent of a raised finger at the beast.

Half deafened, we went along to the shop. The blackboard advertising Rockstar Chianti was still outside, as were two cars, one with French plates, and the other an Italian-registered BMW saloon.

As we opened the door, a chime announced our arrival, but nobody looked up. Inside the shop, there was a female member of staff dealing with the French visitors and a man taking bottles of wine out of a carton and stacking them on solid wooden shelves. The labels indicated that these were 'Special Vintage Rockstar Chianti'. I hoped this was better than the one we had tried. Virgilio walked over to him.

'Good afternoon, are you the manager?'

The man straightened up and took a good hard look at us, probably realising that we weren't here to buy his wine. 'Yes.' A bit less aggressive than Renzi's mongrel, but not exactly warm and welcoming.

Virgilio held out his warrant card and introduced himself, but the manager looked underwhelmed. 'What do you want? I already answered a load of questions on Tuesday.'

'You may not have heard, Signor Mancini, but there have been three more murders at the hotel today.'

'So...?'

I was rapidly taking a dislike to Signor Mancini. Considering that a dead man had been found only about ten metres from where we were standing and three more a short distance away, I found his lack of enthusiasm to cooperate puzzling and potentially suspicious. He was probably in his mid to late fifties like me, but his dark hair had a whole lot less grey in it than mine. He had a hard face and I was immediately reminded of a number of most unpleasant criminals I had encountered in the course of my career with the same look. This was one of those faces that had probably smiled so little in its life, it would now find it a struggle to even attempt a hint of good cheer. Little wonder that Giovanni the postman's old auntie was scared of him. Virgilio continued.

'Where were you on Tuesday between one-thirty and four-thirty?'

'Here.'

'Here, where? In the shop or somewhere else?'

'How am I supposed to remember? I would have been in the shop, in my office or out back in the storeroom.'

I frowned. If I'd been working somewhere so close to a murder, I felt sure I would have been able to pinpoint my movements exactly. Mancini's vagueness bothered me. Did this indicate guilt?

Clearly, Virgilio felt the same way because he adopted a harder tone.

'This is a murder investigation, Signor Mancini. I would advise you to think very carefully and be more specific. I'm going to interview the other members of staff and I'm sure they'll be able to remember where they were and where you were.'

Mancini grunted but did at least provide a more detailed answer. 'Renzi was out in the vineyard and Elena was working in the storeroom.' He pointed towards a door in the far wall. 'I was manning the shop but I also had stuff to do in my office, so I was in and out each time I heard the bell at the door.'

'Did you see a big truck go past out on the road?' Mancini shook his head so Virgilio tried again. 'I understand you were expecting a delivery of boxes on Tuesday – did a truck come here that afternoon?'

'Yes.'

'Why didn't you say so?'

The expression on Mancini's face was smugly insolent and I felt my hackles rise. 'You asked me if I'd seen a truck go past. The answer is no. A truck pulled in here, but it didn't drive past.'

I was impressed to see Virgilio let this wash over him. 'What time did the delivery of boxes happen?'

This time, it appeared that Mancini did at least make an attempt to remember. 'Just after two. He was here for ten minutes or so and then he left.'

Virgilio took down the name of the company responsible for the delivery before pressing him on the truck White claimed to have seen. 'I believe you had a fuel delivery that afternoon. A large fuel tanker was seen parked alongside the cantina just after two. Does that sound familiar?'

Mancini's expression was fascinating. It went from shock to bewilderment and then to contrition. 'Yes. Please excuse me, I forgot about that. We had a delivery of diesel in readiness for next week when all the machinery will be hard at work. Just like I should be if you weren't wasting my time.' His insolent expression returned and, with it, so did my suspicions.

Virgilio gave him a sceptical look. 'Anything else you've forgotten to tell us?' Mancini, still looking smug, shook his head and Virgilio carried on. 'A man was murdered and his body was run over right outside your establishment. You've just told me that you were in and out of this sales area all afternoon. Surely you must have seen something through these lovely big windows.'

'No, like I told your officers on Tuesday, I saw nothing, heard nothing and I certainly didn't murder anybody.'

'It's very convenient that your CCTV wasn't working. Is that something that happens often?' Virgilio's tone was sceptical.

'Now and then. Technology, huh?' It sounded as though Mancini's opinion of technology was no better than his opinion of the police.

'The victim was a journalist. Can you think of any reason why he might have been snooping around here?'

'None whatsoever.' Mancini shook his head just a little bit too emphatically for me. Did this man know more than he was letting on? Virgilio asked him again but received the same reply so he moved on.

'I understand that you have three people working for you here at the winery. Is that correct?'

'Yes, Guido Renzi, Elena Montaione and Mauro Delvecchio. When the *vendemmia* starts next week, there will be four more temporary staff, but for now it's just us.'

'What was Mauro Delvecchio doing on Tuesday afternoon?'

'I have no idea. Probably sleeping. He'd been unwell so he took a couple of days off. He should be back tomorrow.'

'So he wasn't here on Tuesday?'

'He was here first thing, but he was sick that lunchtime and I sent him home.'

'Who else has been murdered?'

Mancini looked genuinely surprised. 'Why? Has somebody else been murdered?'

'Just answer the question, please. Where were you earlier today?'

'Here, working, just like now. If you don't believe me, ask Elena.'

At that moment, the French tourists left the shop with a carton of bottles and Virgilio closed his notebook. 'I will. Thank you for your cooperation.' He handed Mancini one of his cards. 'If you should remember anything useful, please give me a call.'

Mancini took the card, ostentatiously dropped it onto the counter without looking at it and returned to his bottle-stacking. I glanced at Virgilio and saw him roll his eyes. What was it about the people here at the winery?

We walked over to the female employee, and Oscar, who had kept well away from both Guido Renzi and the manager, wandered across to lean against her leg, producing an answering smile from her. She was probably only in her twenties but she had a careworn face. I imagined that working for a sullen boss like Mancini couldn't be a bundle of fun. Unlike the others, she produced a cordial greeting.

'Hello, gentlemen, are you interested in trying our Chianti?'

'Thank you but we're with the police. We're investigating the murder that took place here on Tuesday. I'm Commissario Pisano of the Florence murder squad. Are you Elena Montaione?'

She nodded and had the decency to produce an expression of

sorrow. 'That poor man. How awful to be run over like that.' She looked across at us. 'And it really was murder, was it, not an accident?'

Virgilio didn't mince his words. 'The man was strangled first. He was already dead when the truck ran over him.'

Elena's face paled visibly. 'But who could do such a thing? Who was he?'

'He was an English journalist. Can you think of any reason he might have had to come here?'

I was mildly surprised to see her immediately nod again. 'The American, I bet he came here to spy on the American.' Realising what she'd said, she was quick to qualify her statement. 'But I'm not saying Signor Digger would have killed anybody. I've met him a few times now and he's always struck me as a kind, gentle man – surprising really for a rock star. You know, they do have a bit of a reputation, don't they?' She used the English term 'rock star' but that was presumably because she knew it from their wine.

Virgilio exchanged glances with me before carrying on. 'You can't think of any other reason the victim might have had for being here?'

'No, none at all.'

Virgilio went on to check where she'd been on Tuesday afternoon and the answer was the same as all the others had given. She hadn't seen or heard anything but she explained that she'd been working in the storeroom, which had no windows. She had effectively been secluded from events, as had her male colleague, Mauro Delvecchio. Guido Renzi had allegedly been out in the vines, so the only person here at the winery who might have seen what happened on Tuesday afternoon had been the surly manager.

And it was pretty clear that we weren't going to get anything out of him.

17

THURSDAY AFTERNOON

Outside the shop, Virgilio and I stopped to take stock, and he was the first to pass judgement on the people we'd seen. 'Not exactly a warm welcome from Signor Mancini. I thought the guy with the dog could have been more helpful, but Mancini was a lot worse; he all but told us to get stuffed.' He used one of the many lurid Tuscan expressions that rendered the idea perfectly – although unprintably – and I was in full agreement.

'My friend Giovanni, the postman in Montevolpone, already told me about Mancini. He said he treats his staff like dirt and makes the life of the old lady in the cottage over there a misery. He's definitely not going to win any popularity contests any time soon. I feel sorry for Elena in the shop. Working for somebody like Mancini must be tough. I'm surprised Digger employs him.'

Virgilio nodded a couple of times as he scanned his notebook. 'So what do we think? The three staff members were conveniently disposed of on Tuesday so anybody could have come into the shop and anything could have gone on outside without them knowing. We've now had confirmation that White's story of seeing a fuel tanker was correct, so maybe his account of seeing Greenbank is also true. Mancini has dark hair so could he be our murderer?'

'It wouldn't surprise me, but that brings us back to motive again. What possible motive could the manager of a winery have had for murdering an English journalist? One way or another, it always seems to come back to the three would-be Mafia bosses up at the hotel. Maybe Greenbank was murdered by one of them or one of the bodyguards because of something he'd seen, and maybe they put pressure on Mancini to fake a hit-and-run accident.'

Virgilio let this scenario sink in for a few seconds. 'When you say pressure, what kind of pressure? Mancini doesn't strike me as the kind of guy who would respond to threats. Could he have been in on it with them?'

At that moment, his phone started ringing and a short conversation ensued. When it ended, he pointed up the hill. 'I need to get back to the hotel. Marco and Dini have been interviewing Florida Froot's boyfriend, Johnny Riccio. They say he looks suspicious and, in particular, the CCTV footage shows that he arrived back at just before midday, so he was around when Rossini was strangled. Marco wants me to interview him as well. You're welcome to join in if you like, or maybe you should get back to Anna.'

I checked my watch. It was almost three. 'I'm all right for a few more hours. Talking of CCTV, what about White's story of being outside on the terrace at the time of Rossini's death?'

'It turns out he was telling the truth. The footage shows that he was sitting out there all the time.'

'What are you going to do with him? He's supposed to be flying home tonight. If you want to keep him here, I imagine you'll have to charge him.'

'To be honest, I'm tempted to let him go. Now that I've seen the people down here at the winery, it wouldn't surprise me if White really did see something shady going on, and the shoes in the waste bin are all too obvious. I think somebody's been trying to frame him. I'll talk to Marco – it is his case, after all – but I can't see that we have grounds to charge White, so I think we have to release him.'

I glanced at the little cottage across the road and saw the lace curtains on one of the windows twitch. 'You go up to the hotel, and I'll come along a bit later. I think I'll go and have another few words with the old lady who lives on the other side of the road. When I spoke to her yesterday, I got the feeling she maybe knew more than she was telling me. All right with you?'

* * *

Oscar and I went over to the cottage and, as before, the door opened before we got there. The old lady peered out at us and a look of recognition appeared on her face. 'Oh, it's you. Have you been questioning Signor Mancini?'

I gave her a friendly smile and Oscar wandered over to nuzzle her knees, bringing a smile to her face as well. 'Good afternoon. I didn't realise you were Giovanni's aunt. He's a good friend of mine in Montevolpone.'

'I'm his great-aunt and he's told me all about you. You're the man who solved those awful murders at the golf course last year, aren't you?'

Clearly, Giovanni's bush telegraph worked in both directions. 'I sometimes help the police, especially when English speakers are involved. Could you spare me a few minutes of your time to answer some questions?'

I saw her eyes flit across to the winery shop before she opened the door fully. 'Yes, of course, do come in and I'll make some coffee.' I noticed that she was quick to close the door behind me. Could it be that she'd been given instructions by Mancini not to speak to the police?

Oscar and I followed her into a small living room with polished terracotta tiles on the floor that looked as though they'd been there forever. Some were cracked, some were very worn, but the overall impression was delightful, positively exuding a sense of history. I mentioned this to her and she nodded proudly, drawing my attention to the stone mantelpiece. On the front of this I could just make out the date: 1599. My own little house is over two hundred years old, but this one was twice as old as that. While Giovanni's great-aunt went off to the kitchen to make the coffee, I studied the photographs on the mantelpiece and soon picked out a couple of shots of a much younger Giovanni with his cousins.

'Would you like a bit of cake? I've been baking.' Her voice came from the kitchen and Oscar immediately set off in that direction, no doubt believing the offer to have been made to him. As already established, his linguistic comprehension is excellent when people are talking about food.

Inside the traditional kitchen, we chatted about the weather like a couple of English people while a battered little coffee pot came to the boil. Auntie Linda – who told me her proper name was Linda Ducci – set two small cups on the table and produced a large, ring-shaped cake. This, she told me, was an apple cake made with the addition of polenta flour. The lifebelt shape was down to the circular mould in which it had been baked. She cut two slices – mine twice the size of hers – and was about to put the knife down when there was a plaintive yelp from the floor. We both looked down to see Oscar giving a moving performance as a poor unloved and underfed wretch. Considering he had had his lunch little more than an hour earlier, I was impressed at his thespian talent – and his little act worked. Auntie Linda cut a generous slice of cake and served it to him on a saucer. I had barely had a chance to take a mouthful of mine before he had wolfed down his whole helping.

We sat down at the kitchen table and I gradually brought the conversation around to the death on Tuesday. I asked her if she had remembered anything more and she shook her head, but I felt sure I could see hesitation, so I tried a few supplementary questions.

'How long have you lived here, Signora Ducci?'

'Fifty-seven years. My husband – poor soul – worked here all his life until he passed away six years ago.' She shook her head sadly. 'Maybe it was for the best because the marquis sold the estate to the American a year later and things have never been the same since.'

'Do you see much of the American?'

She shook her head. 'I've only seen him twice since he bought the estate five years ago.'

'So would I be right in thinking that it's Mr Mancini from the winery that you deal with?'

'That's right...' Her voice tailed off and I gave her a gentle push.

'I've just been interviewing him with the *commissario* and I'm afraid I didn't take to him at all. He was downright rude and, considering there's just been a murder close by, he was very uncooperative. Do you find him easy to get on with?'

There was a long pause before she answered. 'Don't you go telling him, but I think he's an awful man. I really can't understand why the American employs him.'

This was a familiar refrain by now so I just nodded and let her carry on.

'If ever I try to complain about noise or even just ask for some work to be done on the cottage – the roof's been leaking for two years now – he threatens to kick me out.' She gave me a beseeching look. 'How can he do that to me after fifty-seven years?'

Oscar, having finished his cake and having polished the floor all around the now spotless saucer, looked up and reacted to her distressed tone by trotting over to settle himself alongside her with his nose on her lap while I rescued the plate from the floor. As she stroked his ears, I reflected on what Auntie Linda had just said and my opinion of Mancini took another nosedive but, I reminded myself, just because he was an unpleasant human being didn't necessarily make him a killer.

I finished my cake and sipped the powerful black coffee as I did my best to get her to reveal whatever it was I felt sure she was failing to disclose, but each time, she just shook her head and repeated her mantra that her hearing and her eyesight weren't what they used to be. When I left there a few minutes later, I still couldn't shift the idea that she knew more than she was saying and I had a shrewd idea that the reason for her hesitation was fear of a man called Mancini.

On the way back up the track to the hotel, I got a phone call from Sergeant Dini.

'Hello, Dan, I've just seen that weird PA – you know, the one who looks after Digger. He tells me Digger would like to have a word with you. Could you spare the time?'

'Yes, of course. By the way, has Marco interviewed him about what he was doing on Tuesday afternoon?'

'Yes and the man confirms he took Digger and his daughter to the Uffizi and then came back again. He spent the afternoon in the apartment, doing his boss's mail – answering fan letters and so on. The chambermaid confirms that he was there so the inspector says we can discount him.'

'Thanks, tell him I'll be there in ten minutes.'

I spent the rest of the walk wondering what the old rocker might have to tell me.

When I arrived in the hotel lobby, I found the 'weird PA' waiting for me by the lift. He greeted Oscar and me with a formal bow and ushered us into what he called the elevator, revealing his transatlantic origins. I would have called it a lift. When we reached the top floor, he escorted us along a different corridor and out through a pair of French windows to a charming rooftop terrace. This was on the shaded side of the villa and there was a hint of a breeze up here, making it more than pleasant. The old rocker was sitting by an amazing old fountain where water gushed into a little pool from the mouth of a beautifully carved stone dolphin. Presumably, the water was on a continuous loop, otherwise it didn't bode well for the rooms below. When Digger saw me, he gave me a lazy wave of the hand.

'Hi there, thanks for coming. Drink?'

'Thanks, but I've drunk quite enough for today.'

He waved me into a chair opposite him and I settled down to hear what he had to say.

'I know you're English, but I forgot your name. Nothing personal, I have a problem with names these days.'

'My name's Dan Armstrong. I'm a Brit but I live in Tuscany now and I sometimes help the local police if there are English speakers involved.'

The answer appeared to please him. 'So you aren't actually part of the Italian police?' I shook my head and he continued, his voice now noticeably lower. We were alone on the terrace. Even Stokes, the PA, had withdrawn, and it was clear that Digger wanted to keep this confidential. 'Listen, Dan, I'd like to have a quiet word in your ear. It's about Johnny, you know, Florida's man.'

'Has he done something wrong?'

'I'm not sure, but it wouldn't surprise me. He's a funny character, half Italian, half French and, to be perfectly honest, I wouldn't trust him as far as I could throw him. Florrie seems to like him, but I don't think it's that serious, but with everything that's happened in the last couple of days, there's something I need to tell you.' We both leant forward and I noticed that even Oscar pricked up his ears. 'He's done time.'

'He has a criminal record?' This was potentially serious.

'He spent four years in jail in Marseille for drug trafficking.'

'How do you know this? Did he tell you?'

He shook his head. 'He didn't breathe a word of it to me or to her. When she first introduced him to me, I didn't like what I saw, so I got him checked out by a private investigation agency. They called me back this lunchtime with preliminary details of his background.' He caught my eye and added a few words of explanation. 'Since Rosie, my wife, died four years ago, Florrie's all I've got left. Stokes thinks I'm overly possessive, but her wellbeing and happiness are the most important things in the world for me, and the idea of her getting herself shacked up with a character like Johnny frightens the life out of me.'

I sat back and reflected on what I'd just heard. I remembered hearing of the death of Digger's wife. She had also been a famous singer in her time and I'd been surprised to learn that they'd been married for something like thirty-five years – which is pretty good going anywhere, let alone in the world of rock 'n' roll. When Marco had called Virgilio, he had indicated that Johnny had looked suspicious and this new information from Digger more than confirmed that first impression. Mention of drugs made me reconsider the whole series of events of the last few days. Might there be a narcotics connection in all this? And, if that proved to be the case, might Florida's boyfriend be behind what had happened?

Keeping my own voice low as well, I formulated a response. 'Thank you for telling me this. I'll pass all the information to the inspector in charge of the investigation. I know him well now and he's a good man. He won't say a word to your daughter and I certainly won't either. To be honest, it's standard practice with suspects in a murder case to check for a criminal record, so it would have come out anyway sooner or later.'

He pounced on my choice of words. 'You said "suspects" – does this mean you consider him a suspect in these awful murders?'

'Who knows? He's being interviewed by the *commissario* as we speak.'

'That's good to know. Thank you for your time, Dan.' He produced a little grin. 'And if the *commissario* were to mention to Florrie that a check of police files had revealed Johnny's record, you wouldn't hear me complaining.'

18

THURSDAY AFTERNOON

As soon as I got back downstairs, I looked for Marco or Virgilio but was told that they were still interviewing Johnny Riccio. I found Sergeant Dini outside and told her what Digger had just said, suggesting that she slip into the interview room and pass on the information about Johnny's criminal past to her boss. She headed off and I wandered around to the terrace, where I took a seat at a table under a parasol with Oscar settled happily at my feet. I ordered a low-alcohol beer and had been sitting there for only a couple of minutes when my attention was drawn to a scene down at the pool.

A man and a woman were having a furious argument, and I realised that the couple in question were Matthew White and my ex-wife. I looked on in silent fascination as I tried to imagine what they were saying – or, rather, shouting – at each other. I saw heads turned towards them as the row disturbed other guests down at the pool, but from where I was sitting, I couldn't make out what was being said. What was clear, however, was that they were going at it hammer and tongs.

The shouting match lasted for several minutes before White

stormed off, leaving Helen standing on her own with a number of spectators staring at her. Unsurprisingly, she hastily collected her things and came back towards the villa. As she climbed the steps to the terrace, she spotted me and made her way across to my table. I gave her a smile but I didn't feel much like smiling. Seeing her in full Furies mode had brought back painful memories of the final months of our marriage. Doing my best to dismiss the flashback, I felt morally obliged to point to the spare chair at my table.

'Come and have a sit down. You look as if you could do with a drink.'

'Thanks, but I don't want any more alcohol. I just need to sit quietly for a bit.' She sat down and was joined by Oscar, who had decided to offer her a bit of canine support. After stroking his ears for a few moments, she shot me a quick glance. 'I suppose you saw what just happened?'

'It didn't look very pleasant. Do I take it that your relationship with Matthew White is now officially over?'

'And how! He came storming out five minutes ago and accused me of ratting on him to the police. He said that it was all my fault that he'd been arrested. I thought he was going to hit me at one point.'

She subsided into disgruntled silence while I carried on sipping my beer, wondering how long I should stay with her. I could well imagine White's anger at being handcuffed and interrogated, but surely after lying to the police twice about his movements on Tuesday afternoon, he had only himself to blame. Fortunately, my phone started ringing and I saw that it was Virgilio.

'*Ciao*, Dan, have you got a minute?'

Suppressing a feeling of relief, I answered willingly. 'Of course, where are you?'

'Outside the front door.'

'I'll come right away.'

I swallowed the last of my beer and gave Helen an apologetic look. 'I'm sorry but the *commissario* wants to see me urgently. Don't worry, at least you're free of that man now.'

'Thanks, Dan...' Her voice tailed off miserably and I almost stayed with her, but common sense asserted itself and I called Oscar and headed off.

Virgilio, Marco and Dini were sitting on the familiar stone bench at the edge of the vineyard and I joined them there, all four of us facing out over the rows of vines. I was quick to ask how the interview with Johnny had gone and Marco answered first.

'Thanks for passing on that information about his time in prison. I would have done a check anyway because the guy just didn't strike me as on the level, but it was good to know in advance. Naturally, he claims he's a reformed character, mainly as a result of the love of a good woman – he says Florida, but who knows?'

'Do you think he might be our murderer?'

'I wouldn't put it past him. He's big enough to have strangled Greenbank or the bodyguard. Bashing the others over the head wouldn't have been a problem and, as far as I can tell, he has no alibi for the time of Rossini's murder this morning. He claims to have been at a wine auction in Greve in Chianti and he returned from his trip at a quarter to twelve, so he was here at the villa with access to all areas. As far as the murders in the vineyard last night are concerned, he claims to have been tucked up in bed with Florida but, of course, the same applies to him as we said about your ex-wife: he could have drugged her with Rohypnol and she wouldn't remember a thing.'

Virgilio took up the conversation. 'He's certainly on my list of possibles, but we come back to the same old problem of motive. What possible motive could a wine-buying playboy have for murdering a bunch of almost certainly Mafia hoods? I can't see what would make him do something like that, not least as it would have been a bit too close to home. After all, he's now found himself a very wealthy girlfriend so why commit multiple murders on her, or rather her father's, doorstep?' He sounded deeply frustrated, and so was I.

'I know what you mean, Virgilio. I've been struggling to come up with a convincing motive for any of the murders. What we're saying is that we have a number of suspects with opportunity – with or without the help of Rohypnol – and means, but no clear motive unless one of them is a professional hitman, sent from Puglia. By the way, any joy with Oscar's piece of wood?'

'It's gone to the lab along with fingerprints and DNA samples of the main suspects but it'll probably be a few hours before we get a result. In the meantime, I've sent a couple of men down to the winery to take prints and DNA samples from the staff there, particularly the unlikeable Signor Mancini.' He turned towards me and gave me a wry smile. 'You never know, we may get lucky.'

'Who *are* the main suspects?' I carried straight on, counting them off on my fingers. 'There's Davide Cassano and either or both of the two remaining bodyguards. Add in Johnny Riccio, and Mancini at the winery. That makes five. Have I missed anybody out? What about the English writer? By the way, I see that you've released Matthew White. Are you letting him get on his flight home tonight?'

Marco answered. 'There's no way we can keep him here, and the same applies to Ogilvie, the writer. I can't see them as being professional hitmen and I'm unable to come up with any viable motive for either, so I think we just wash our hands of them. So, yes, that means we're left with five possible suspects and, the way things are at the moment, not a shred of evidence against any of them unless Oscar's lump of wood provides us with a match.'

'The Rohypnol bottle in the third bodyguard's toilet? What was his name... Torchio?'

'Arturo Torchio. I think it's almost certain that it was deliberately put there to frame him, just like the shoes were dropped in White's waste bin. Disinformation.'

I nodded. 'On that basis, if we remove Torchio from the frame, we're left with just four suspects. What about the first murder? I'm still not convinced that the four are connected although the proximity of the murders is certainly suspicious. Did you hear back from the haulage company that delivered the carboard boxes?'

The sergeant answered this time. 'The delivery was logged at five past two on Tuesday, and the driver says he saw nothing unusual. It was the manager himself who signed for the delivery.'

'And the fuel tanker that White claims to have seen?'

'Our people down at the winery now are getting the manager to give us the name of the fuel company, so we can double-check White's story. No word yet, but that should be pretty quick.'

I addressed myself to Marco. 'Is there anything more I can do here? If not, I think I'd better get back home.'

'You go off, Dan. I'm sorry I spoiled your romantic day with Anna. Thank you for all your help. We really appreciate it.'

Virgilio clapped me on the shoulder. 'Absolutely. Thanks a lot, Dan. Go off and enjoy the rest of the day.'

I stood up and Oscar got up as well, stretched and looked up at me. I shook hands with the three of them and asked them to keep me informed of any developments, hoping there would be some. I set off across the car park to my van and almost got run over by a white Fiat that came shooting past, churning up the gravel with its wheels. Luckily, Oscar was still sniffing one of the big umbrella pines and was well out of the way. Interestingly, the driver of the car was none other than Matthew White, and I saw that the passenger seat alongside him was empty. I was still digesting the significance of this when I heard someone call my name.

'Dan, can you help?'

I turned to see Helen coming towards me and, even from a distance, I could see that she was upset. As she approached, it was clear that she was crying, and I spontaneously opened my arms and caught her in a comforting hug.

'It's all right, Helen, everything's okay again now.'

Her voice when she answered was partly muffled by my shoulder. 'I wish it was. He's gone off and left me. How am I supposed to get to the airport now?'

Florence airport is close to the city and only forty-five minutes or so from where we were. I glanced at my watch and saw that it was almost half past four. 'What time's your flight?'

'Six-fifty, but I really need to be at the airport a couple of hours before.'

I didn't really want to, but I couldn't see any alternative. 'I'm heading in that direction now. I can take you. Where's your bag?' No sooner had I spoken than I found myself wondering whether I was going to regret making this offer. After telling Anna that I never expected to see Helen again, here I was actively inviting her into my company. Was this fair on Anna? Should I have left Helen to her own devices? Was I somehow being unfaithful to my wonderful partner?

Helen squeezed me even harder. 'Oh, Dan, I'm so sorry to bother you. Won't it take you out of your way?' She finally released the pressure on my ribs and stepped back. 'I'm sure the hotel could call me a taxi.' She was offering me a way out but, stupidly, I didn't take it. Maybe this was for old times' sake, or maybe because she was looking so vulnerable, but I decided to go ahead and give her a lift. Apart from anything else, it would hasten her departure from Tuscany and from my life.

'It probably wouldn't get here for half an hour or more. Don't worry, it's no bother. Now, let's get your bag and we can head off.'

19

THURSDAY AFTERNOON

The drive back started in silence but gradually loosened up as Helen began to relax. I deliberately didn't mention the events of the past few days and, instead, I went into tour-guide mode, telling her all I could remember about the places we passed en route. To be honest, I didn't know much about the historical side of things – that's Anna's domain – but I pointed out a couple of fine old villas tucked in the trees and numerous wineries all preparing for the harvest. I told her it was lucky we were doing this route this week and not next, because I knew from experience that as soon as the *vendemmia* started, the roads would be filled with slow-moving tractors pulling trailers full of grapes. She looked over towards me.

'You're really settled here now, aren't you? Is this where you plan on ending your days?'

I glanced back at her. 'Hopefully not for a good long time, but yes, I really think of Tuscany as my home now. It's got everything: history, culture, beautiful scenery, gorgeous weather and don't let's forget the food and drink.'

'And, of course, we mustn't forget your new lady friend.'

I suddenly found myself concentrating very hard on the road ahead. The conversation was drifting into dangerous territory. I gave no response to her comment but she carried on regardless. 'Do I presume that she was the woman you were with at the hotel?'

I found myself having to clear my throat before answering. 'Yes, her name's Anna.'

'Tricia tells me you've been together for almost a year now. It must be serious.'

By this time, we had reached the main road parallel to the river and I had to stop and wait for an opening in the traffic before pulling out and heading towards Florence. I gave it another minute or two before finally accepting that she was still waiting for an answer.

'It is serious.'

'Do you love her?'

Maybe it's just because I'm a man, or maybe it's the way I was brought up, but I've never been terribly good at expressing feelings – and talking to my ex-wife about my new partner was surely about as tricky as it gets. In the end, after a lot of thought, all I could say was, 'Yes.'

Helen reached across and laid her hand on my thigh. 'Then I'm very happy for you. She's a lucky girl.'

The combination of her hand on my thigh and the unexpected good wishes almost caused me to run into the back of the car in front. Thankfully, she removed her hand almost immediately and changed the subject to our daughter.

'Tricia likes her, so that's good.'

'Tricia came over at Christmas and she and Anna got on really well together.' I babbled on about what we'd done at Christmas, wishing that the airport were closer, until I reached the traffic lights in Lastra a Signa. After what seemed like an interminable silence – that probably lasted barely a minute – the lights changed to green and as we pulled away, my eyes were drawn to a familiar little blue Fiat coming in the opposite direction. At the wheel was Anna, and I felt my blood turn cold. As our two vehicles passed each other, I thought I was going to get away with it but then, at the last moment, I saw her face turn in my direction and comprehension dawn. A second later and she was disappearing in my rear-view mirror, but the damage had been done. I glanced sideways at Helen but, fortunately, she hadn't seen Anna and we were able to spend the next fifteen minutes until we got to the airport talking about trivia – which suited me fine.

It was with considerable relief that I pulled up in the no-parking area outside the terminal building and jumped out to grab her bag from the back seat. As I emerged with it, she reached in past me and patted Oscar's head as he stood up and looked over the seat back.

'Lucky Dan, he's got a best buddy and a beautiful girlfriend.' She sounded wistful and I did my best to offer a few words of encouragement.

'You'll find somebody too – and you could always start by getting a Labrador.'

She reached up and pulled my face down enough so she could kiss me. 'Or a Dan...'

Fortunately, she then picked up her bag, thanked me again, and disappeared through the glass doors. I hastily jumped back into the van and headed out again, determined to go straight home and explain to Anna why it was that she'd seen me with Helen.

Half an hour later, I was bumping up the *strada bianca* towards my house, desperately practising what I was going to say. Only a few hundred metres before the house, I met a pickup coming the other way and pulled into the side to let it past. As he came level with me, the driver stopped and extended his hand towards me through the open window. It was Fausto.

'*Ciao*, Dan. Have you caught the murderer?' We shook hands.

'How did you know I was investigating a murder?' Even as I asked the question, I realised that it was almost certainly rhetorical. 'Have you been talking to our friendly local postman by any chance?'

He grinned at me. 'Giovanni knows everything. Apparently, some poor soul was murdered at the Rockstar winery.'

I made a vain attempt to move the conversation away from murder. 'Have you tasted it? They call it the "Best Chianti in Tuscany" but your wine is head and shoulders better than it.'

'You wouldn't believe how many wine makers advertise their wine as the best in Tuscany, if not the world. So why was the guy at the winery murdered?'

I gave him a helpless look. 'I have no idea. The guy who was murdered was an investigative journalist and from his past work, it looks as though he was investigating a fraud of some kind, but we're at a loss to know what it was.'

'It could be wine, of course.'

Fausto's words stopped me in my tracks.

'Wine? I remember you telling me about the olive oil and salami scams and you mentioned wine. How can you scam people with wine?'

'All sorts of ways. The easy way is to water it down, or some people pour in sacks of sugar at the fermentation stage to make a weak wine stronger but, around here, the obvious thing to do is to bring in cheaper wine from somewhere else and mix them.' Seeing the puzzled look on my face, he elaborated. 'The Podere dei Santi, the Rockstar winery, is in the Montespertoli DOCG area, and the Chianti from there commands a premium. I make

Chianti, but I'm just outside the guaranteed quality area, and so, however good you and I think it is, people aren't prepared to pay over the top for it. If somebody in a DOCG wants to cheat, the easiest thing is to get a tanker full of decent strong wine from somewhere else for less than half the price and mix it with the local stuff.'

The word 'tanker' suddenly set a very loud bell ringing in my head. From the moment that Matthew White had told us about seeing the tanker, he and we had assumed that it must have been a fuel tanker, but maybe it had contained red wine. This would of course explain why Greenbank had been videoing the truck.

And why he'd been murdered.

I thanked Fausto and he gave me a cheery wave and went on his way. As his pickup disappeared down the road, I sat there for a minute or so, contemplating what I needed to do. I had two pressing priorities: I needed to report this to Marco or his boss as soon as possible, but I also had to see Anna to explain the circumstances surrounding the appearance of my ex-wife in my car with me. I was only a short distance from home so I opted to make a quick phone call to Marco and then head straight back to see Anna.

I tried both Marco and Virgilio but without getting an answer. After that, I dug out Sergeant Dini's number and was relieved to hear her voice.

'*Pronto*.'

'Hi, it's Dan Armstrong. Did your officers manage to get the DNA samples from the people at the winery?'

'Good afternoon, Dan. Yes, we got the samples and everything's been sent to the lab.'

'While they were down there, did Signor Mancini let them have the name of the company allegedly delivering fuel on

Tuesday afternoon in a tanker? I'm guessing that the answer is no.'

'You've guessed right. It appears he was unable to locate the invoice or the delivery note but he told the officers that he would keep looking.'

'I think he'll be looking for a long time. I've just been talking to a friend and something has occurred to me.' I went on to quickly outline what I'd heard from Fausto, and Dini reacted enthusiastically.

'That could be it, Dan.' She was sounding animated. 'Maybe Greenbank was investigating a scam involving adulterated wine and he traced it to the Rockstar winery. Somebody with a guilty conscience down there caught him and murdered him to keep him quiet. No prizes for guessing who the most likely perpetrator is.'

'I agree. I think it almost certainly has to be Mancini, although I suppose there might be a question mark hanging over Florida Froot's boyfriend. Maybe Mancini was adulterating the wine and "Johnny" was selling it as authentic DOCG Chianti, knowing full well that it wasn't the real thing. I suppose it's also possible that the whole scam has been orchestrated by Digger, but I doubt it. I think it's more likely that he's also been a victim of the scam. By buying in cheap wine from elsewhere and mixing it, Mancini has increased the output of the winery but probably without telling the owner. That remains to be seen. Anyway, you'd better make sure that the inspector or the *commissario* hear about this as soon as possible. There's something I need to do now, but if Marco or Virgilio want to give me a call, they know how to contact me.'

As soon as I'd finished the call, I started the engine again and carried on up the track to my house. Above me, the sky was now completely covered with sinister-looking dark clouds and it looked as though we were going to get a downpour before long. I just hoped that this wouldn't turn out to be an omen for what awaited me inside. I saw Anna's car parked outside the house and glanced in the rear-view mirror towards the big, black nose looking at me over the top of the rear seat. 'Wish me luck, Oscar.'

For a moment, it looked to me as though he winked.

I found Anna sitting at the kitchen table with her laptop open in front of her. She raised her eyes as I came in and gave me an enquiring look while she reciprocated the enthusiastic greeting from Oscar. 'Something you'd like to tell me, Dan?'

I pulled out a chair and sat down alongside her. 'I've come to explain how it was that Helen ended up in my car with me.'

She closed her laptop and crossed her arms. 'I'm listening.' Her tone wasn't icy, but it wasn't warm and friendly either.

I gave her a full explanation, telling her that I had been on my way back to spend time with her on her birthday but had been waylaid by my ex-wife. I pointed out that the sudden departure of Helen's ex-boyfriend had left her effectively marooned in the country. In consequence, giving her a lift to the airport had seemed like a natural and pragmatic solution. I finished with the words, 'I was going to tell you tonight, but then of course, we saw each other on the road in Lastra, didn't we?'

She nodded a few times before looking me square in the eye. 'I asked you before whether I should be worried. I'm beginning to think maybe I should be. Where is she now?'

I checked my watch. It was past five-thirty. 'Probably in the queue for check-in or security. Her flight leaves just before seven and I know she's desperate to get home.' Anna still didn't look completely reassured so I tried again. 'I've told you before, and I'll say it again, there are only three women in my life and those are you, Tricia, and my mum. This whole Helen hiatus was as much of a shock to me as it was to you, or indeed to Helen, I imagine, but please believe me when I tell you she's out of my life forever and you're in it... hopefully forever.'

I waited anxiously for what seemed like an age before she reached over and gripped my hand in hers. 'All right, you're excused. Knowing you, you probably would have given even a normal suspect a lift to the airport. It's the kind of man you are. Just promise me that I'm not going to find your ex-wife intruding into our relationship any more.'

'You have my word for it. And I meant it when I said "forever".' I reached across the tabletop and caught hold of her hands. 'I've never been so certain about anything in my life.'

20

THURSDAY LATE AFTERNOON

I had just made two cups of tea when my phone started ringing. It was Virgilio.

'*Ciao*, Dan, thanks for the wine-fraud idea. I'm on my way down to the winery at this very moment to talk to Mancini again. I'll get the fraud specialists from Florence to go through his books and, if necessary, I'll get them to compare samples from all of the barrels in the winery. Interestingly, my officers tell me there's a little puddle of wine under one of them that looks very fresh – maybe just delivered.'

'Excellent. I hope you get a result.' I thought I'd better add a few words of caution. 'Of course, this isn't necessarily going to solve the question of who murdered the other three men at the hotel and why.'

'I fear you're right. Just like you said, maybe we need to be looking for two murderers, not one. If Mancini killed Greenbank, that doesn't automatically mean that he killed the others.'

'What about Oscar's lump of wood? Any joy with the DNA?'

'Afraid not. No prints and no DNA, apart from the blood of Bellomo and Calabrese. At least we now know that this was the murder weapon for both of the would-be Mafia big bosses so it makes it more likely that the hotel deaths were all the work of one man. If we take Mancini out of the equation, we're left with the last would be boss, Cassano, or the two remaining body-guards. And don't let's forget Johnny Riccio. Marco and I are going to interview each of them again as soon as we've finished with Mancini. Do you want to come along or are you having an intimate dinner with Anna?'

I glanced up at Anna and saw her watching me as I replied to Virgilio. 'I think I'd rather stay here tonight if you don't mind. I've been in Anna's bad books and I need to make it up to her.'

Anna tapped me on the wrist. 'Dan, don't feel you've got to stay here for my sake if you feel you need to get back to the murders. I've got a heap of work still to do and I'm not in the mood for anything more than a snack tonight, so you go off and try and solve your murders and we can catch up later on.'

'Are you sure?' The difference between Anna's attitude and the fractious final years of my relationship with Helen couldn't have been more stark. I found myself spontaneously reaching down to kiss her neck and she grinned at me.

'Of course I'm sure. I know you well enough by now. Go on.' She raised her voice. 'It's all right, Virgilio, he has my blessing.'

I was already getting to my feet when I felt Oscar's nose give me a couple of prods. I glanced down, wondering what he wanted and, as I did so, I suddenly remembered what I'd almost forgotten. I reached into my pocket for the little packet the jeweller on the Ponte Vecchio had gift-wrapped for me days ago, and slid it across the table towards Anna.

'Happy birthday, Anna. I hope you like it.'

I left her to unwrap it and, as Oscar and I went out of the door, I glanced down at him again. 'Thanks, buddy. I owe you.'

He looked back up with an expression on his face that clearly indicated that he was fully aware of that already, but that a T-bone steak would repay the debt nicely.

By the time I got to the hotel, Virgilio and Marco had started interviewing Mancini down at the winery but, according to Sergeant Dini, they were making slow progress. I felt sure they must be getting very frustrated, but what the sergeant said next gave me an idea.

'If only we had a witness. A murder and then a phoney hit-and-run involving a big truck surely can't be as easy as all that to conceal. Somebody must have seen something.'

She was right. I thanked her and set off down the track to the winery at a run, gradually slowing down as my big lunch reminded me of its presence. Untroubled by gastric discomfort, Oscar ran off into the vines and returned with twigs and branches for me to throw for him as usual. Certainly the vine-yard was a wonderful place for a Labrador as well as for a murderer, although when the expected rain arrived, I knew that it would very quickly tun into a muddy mess and my dog along with it. A glance at the sky told me that a downpour was imminent.

When I got to the winery, I wasted no time and hurried up the path to the front door of Auntie Linda's cottage. This time, I actually managed to reach the door and knock once before it was opened. Auntie Linda smiled when she saw Oscar and even managed a bit of a smile for me, although I could see she was looking nervous. No doubt the two blue and white police cars parked outside the winery were responsible for her unease.

'Good evening. Maybe you can tell me what all the commo-tion's about. What are the police doing in the winery?'

'They're in the process of interviewing Mancini. It seems very likely that he's been committing fraud on a big scale and maybe murder too.' I saw her eyes light up. 'We think he may be mixing good Chianti with cheaper red wine so as to increase his profits and line his own pockets.' I could see she was following very closely so I deliberately upped the ante. 'You know what this means, don't you? This means that Mancini will go to jail but, even more importantly from your point of view, he'll be guaranteed to lose his job. And when he goes, then all your cares and woes will leave with him. I imagine it wouldn't sadden you if he disappeared from your life.'

I was pleased to see a smile appear on her face, this time a broad, genuine smile of pleasure and considerable relief. 'You can't imagine how happy I am to hear you say that. The sooner that horrible man is out of my life, the better.'

'Take it from me that he will very quickly be out of your life.' I leant a little closer to her. 'You won't need to be afraid any longer. He won't be able to do anything to you.' I gave her a moment or two to digest this and then asked the all-important question. 'But we need hard evidence against him. Please can you tell me what you saw on Tuesday afternoon? I know you saw something and I can understand that you've been afraid to speak up.' I mentally crossed my fingers. It had only been an impression I'd gained from speaking to her before. Maybe I was barking up the wrong tree, but I knew I had to try. 'There's no need to be afraid any more. Mancini will no longer be in your hair, and I'm sure you'll be quite safe here in your house for as long as you want to stay. I'm going to see the American later on and I'll make sure he knows how badly you've been treated and I'll tell him about the leaky roof as well. Please, it's very important: what did you see? You did see a big truck, didn't you?'

There was an agonising pause and then she nodded. 'There were two trucks. I recognised one because it was from the packaging people. That's where the winery buys cardboard boxes.'

'Tell me about the other truck.' I tried hard to keep the excitement out of my voice.

'It was one of those tanker trucks.'

'And you know what was in it, don't you?'

'I've suspected Mancini for a couple of years now. Last year, I was chatting to the driver, and it was the same man this time. I speak a bit of French and it was good to use it again.'

'French? Had the truck come from France?'

She nodded. 'He told me he'd come all the way from the Languedoc to make a delivery. He didn't say of what, but I may be old but I'm not stupid. He wasn't transporting lemonade.'

'Can you remember the name of the haulage company?' I knew the Languedoc. Helen and I had spent a camping holiday near Perpignan many years ago when Tricia was little and I remembered it as being only a stone's throw from the Spanish border, way down south.

'No, there was nothing written on the side of the truck, but the driver told me he lived in Carcassonne.'

I recognised the name of the old walled *cité* that we'd visited on the way home in the car. The important thing as far as this investigation was concerned was that it wasn't a very big city, so there were unlikely to be too many road-haulage firms there. I thanked her and tried a different tack.

'You know that a man was run over on Tuesday, don't you? After all, you reported the discovery of the body to the police. I don't suppose you saw anything of what happened, or did you?'

There was a lengthy pause before she finally threw caution to the wind and told me what I'd been hoping to hear. 'I didn't see what happened, but I heard a lot of shouting. The truck driver was furious because somebody from the winery had moved his truck without his permission. I have a feeling that it was while that was going on that that poor man was squashed, accidentally or deliberately.'

'Did you see who was driving the truck when it was moved?'

'No, but the shouting match was between the driver and Signor Mancini. Maybe *he* moved it.'

I thanked her profusely and repeated my promise to speak to Digger about her and her cottage before bidding her farewell and heading across to the winery.

A constable at the door let me in with a salute and pointed towards the office. 'They're still in there, sir, questioning the manager. Do you want to go and join them?'

'I'd actually like a quiet word with the inspector or the *commissario* first.' I tore a page out of my notebook and scribbled seven words on it:

Very important new information. I'm outside. Dan.

The constable went over to the office door, knocked, and went in. Twenty seconds later, he came back out again, followed by Virgilio.

'*Ciao*, Dan. What've you got? We're getting nowhere with Mancini.'

I passed on what Auntie Linda had just told me and his eyes lit up. 'Brilliant. Marco and I've been banging our heads against a brick wall for the last half-hour with Mancini. He just denies everything. The more I listen to him, the more convinced I'm becoming that he's the person who killed Greenbank. Up till now, he knows that we've had no proof against him.' He grinned at me and rubbed his palms together. 'That's about to change. You coming?'

Oscar and I followed him into the office and I saw Mancini

look up at me with a cocky glint in his eye. That only lasted until Virgilio started speaking to one of the two officers flanking him.

'Bosco, I want you to handcuff Signor Mancini.' He transferred his attention to the shocked looking winery manager as the cuffs were fitted. 'Fabiano Mancini, I'm arresting you for fraud and the suspected murder of Anthony Greenbank. You will be taken to the *questura* in Florence where you will be held until the public prosecutor decides the date of your trial.'

'But, but, murder? I haven't committed murder.' Mancini was looking far from cocky now. Interestingly, I noted that he didn't deny committing fraud. 'You can't pin that man's death on me. I didn't do it and, besides, you don't have any evidence.'

I saw Marco looking puzzled and shot him a surreptitious wink while his boss ratcheted up the pressure on the winery manager.

'Let's start with the easy one: fraudulent wine sales. We now know that on Tuesday afternoon, you took delivery of a tanker full of wine from the Languedoc region of France. The driver lives in Carcassonne and he's giving the French police a statement as I speak. Think very carefully before you answer: do you still deny mixing the DOCG Chianti produced here with wine of a lesser value so as to defraud your customers and your employer? Well, do you deny it?'

I liked the fact that Virgilio had invented the story of the truck driver already being questioned and I studied Mancini's face carefully. I was delighted to see that his expression was one I recognised from my days in the Met. It was a mixture of shock at being found out, helplessness at finding himself faced with irrefutable evidence and, finally, surrender. His shoulders slumped and he nodded a couple of times.

'All right, I admit it. I wasn't doing any harm to anybody. It's good wine that I've been bringing in from France and when I mix it with our own Chianti, the result is barely distinguishable from the Chianti itself.' That wasn't the way I remembered it, but I made no comment as Virgilio continued.

'But it could no longer be sold as a wine guaranteed as coming from this area, so that makes it fraud. Good, I'm glad you've seen reason at last and have finally realised that the only way you can help yourself is by telling us the truth. Now for the more serious charge: I put it to you that on Tuesday afternoon, you strangled Anthony Greenbank and then staged a hit-and-run accident by deliberately driving the French tanker over the man's body. Is that how it happened or have I got some of it wrong?'

'That wasn't me. I wouldn't kill anybody. Besides, I've never driven a truck in my life.'

He sounded pretty convincing but considering how unforthcoming he'd been up till now, I wasn't taking it at face value. I remembered what Paul in London had told me and reminded Mancini of it. 'A few weeks ago, when you found out that you had an investigative journalist on your trail, you sent him threatening messages to deter him and, when that didn't work, you killed him. Right?'

'No, that's not right. How could I send messages to somebody I didn't know? You're all wrong. I didn't kill anybody. You have to believe me.'

Marco joined in. 'And your killing spree didn't stop there, did it? There have been three more murders up at the hotel and you were responsible for all of them, weren't you?' Mancini started shaking his head but Marco pressed on. 'Tell us why you killed them, Mancini. Are you involved with the Mafia, by any chance?'

The look that spread across Mancini's face was one of horror. 'Me, Mafia? Are you out of your mind?'

'So you're saying you had nothing to do with those latest murders?'

'No, nothing at all. I don't even know who you're talking about and I didn't murder anybody down here either. You have to believe me.'

This time, I found myself beginning to believe the man. He looked genuinely stunned.

Virgilio was losing patience by now and he gave Mancini a dismissive glare before turning to the two constables. 'Take him back to the *questura* and lock him up. Maybe a few nights in the cells will loosen his tongue.'

21

THURSDAY EVENING

After Mancini had been led away, we looked at each other. Marco was the first to speak, asking me who had produced the evidence of the arrival of the French truck. When I told him it had been Auntie Linda, he looked impressed.

'Well done, Dan. I spent half an hour with her yesterday and I couldn't get anything out of her. I don't suppose she saw the actual murder, did she?'

'No, but her confirmation of the tanker story makes it more likely that White was telling us the truth.' Thoughts of Matthew White reminded me of Helen. A glance at my watch told me that she would probably be boarding the aircraft around now and I wondered if she would find herself having to sit next to White. At least, I told myself, it now looked pretty definite that she wouldn't be sitting next to a murderer.

Virgilio's voice shook me out of my thoughts.

'I tended to believe Mancini when he denied involvement in the three murders at the hotel. As for the death of the journalist, who knows if he did that? Dini, get onto the French police and ask them to trace the haulage company in or near Carcassonne.

Ask them to take a statement from the driver and see if they can swab the cab for DNA or fingerprints belonging to anybody else. And check his licence and background to see if he maybe has driven big trucks before. Certainly Mancini had a lot to lose if the wine story ever got out to the media, but I can't see any connection between him and our Mafia friends, can you?'

'Have the *Antimafia* people been contacted about him?'

Sergeant Dini answered me. 'Yes, earlier this afternoon, and we also asked them to check Johnny Riccio, Florida Froot's boyfriend. No response yet.'

'Right, I need to get back to the hotel.' I was pleased to hear Marco take control of the investigation again. Having his boss and a retired English copper butting in from time to time couldn't have made it easy for him, and I could sympathise. He picked up his notebook and pen and looked around at us. 'I agree that it looks unlikely that Mancini was involved with the murders at the hotel, but I still think he killed Greenbank, mainly because if he didn't kill him, then who did? Here's hoping we get something helpful back from the Carcassonne police. We're left with four suspects up at the hotel and I want to interview them all again.' He glanced at Virgilio and me. 'Who's coming?'

I was the first to respond. 'The last thing I want is to horn in on your investigation, Marco, but I wouldn't mind being able to sit in on the interview with Florida's boyfriend. I haven't met him yet and I'd be very interested to see what it is about him that makes you feel he's suspicious.'

'Of course, Dan, and do feel free to speak up if you have any questions for him.' He turned towards Virgilio. 'What about you, sir? Are you coming?'

Virgilio shook his head. 'No, you're in charge. You can handle that. I need to go back to Florence to speak to the public prosecutor about Mancini, and he's bound to ask me for a progress report on the other murders, so I'll look after that side of things for you, Marco, and save you some time. All right?'

'Please do. The prosecutor frightens the life out of me.' Marco stood up and Oscar immediately jumped to his feet as well. 'Feel like a run in the vineyard, Oscar?'

He did.

On the way up the track to the hotel, in between lobbing sticks for Oscar to retrieve, Marco and I discussed the questions we needed to put to the suspects and decided to start with Johnny Riccio. After that, I would leave Marco and Dini to it and return home to Anna. I asked Marco what it had been about Johnny that had looked suspicious. He subcontracted the answer to the sergeant, who was looking less nervous now as she gradually found her feet in the investigative team.

'The first impression I got, the moment Riccio walked in the door, was of a phoney. Maybe it's just a female reaction, but there was something slimy about him. Underneath the expensive clothes and the immaculate hairstyle, I felt sure there was a fundamentally untrustworthy person lurking there. I haven't met his girlfriend, but I'm amazed that any woman could go for a slimy toad like him. He genuinely made my skin creep.'

I smiled at her. 'I get the picture and I got the impression Florida's father feels the same way about Johnny Riccio. But, apart from his creepiness, what was it about him that made you think he's the kind to commit murder?'

She waited until I'd picked up a particularly long branch that Oscar had deposited at my feet and thrown it up the track for him before she answered. 'As you'll see, Riccio's a big, strong man, so I'm sure he wouldn't have had any difficulty in committing the crimes, but it was his background that concerned me more than anything.'

'In what way?'

'No formal education, no steady job – although he describes himself as a wine merchant, he has no office or staff – but he still dresses like a film star and drives around in a Lamborghini. Where does all his money come from?'

I hazarded a guess. 'Does he make a habit of dating rich heiresses like Florida? Maybe he has a whole string of previous girlfriends who've been only too happy to keep him in expensive clothes and flashy cars?'

Marco nodded in agreement. 'We were wondering the same thing, but I wouldn't rule out Riccio getting his money by even more devious means. Maybe he was in on the wine scam with Mancini. Alternatively, what if he's a killer for hire who came here to carry out a contract to kill the three plotters?'

I turned that scenario over in my head. 'Well, Digger has told us that Riccio has a criminal record – and he was in the drugs trade, which is notoriously violent – so it could be he's branched out into contract killings. Since coming here, this would mean he's killed two of the three would-be mafiosi plus a bodyguard. If he really is a hitman, then Cassano's probably right to be scared stiff of being the next victim.'

The sergeant looked dubious. 'But with the hotel crawling with police officers, would Riccio really risk carrying out another murder?'

'I don't know. I suppose it would depend on the terms of the contract. Maybe he only gets paid if all three are liquidated. When you're interviewing Cassano, make sure he's under no illusions about being in a very dangerous situation, whoever the murderer is.'

We were almost at the hotel when a blinding flash of lightning and an almost simultaneous clap of thunder made us jump. It had been getting steadily darker under the leaden sky and the pyrotechnics even made Oscar drop his latest stick. Seconds later, it started to rain, but this wasn't gentle English rain. This was a downpour so strong that it was as if a tap had been turned on. We ran the rest of the way to the entrance but, even so, we were brushing the water off our heads and shoulders when we got there, and Oscar was shaking himself – mercifully out of range of any of the guests. Another two minutes and we would have been soaked to the skin. Looking back, it was hard to see across the car park through a curtain of water so intense that when the drops hit the ground, they bounced back up off the dry gravel again. The noise was like being in a car wash. When it rains in Tuscany, it *rains*.

A constable was standing in the lobby, and Oscar and I followed Marco and Sergeant Dini across to him. 'Where are Cassano, Fosca and Torchio?'

'Most probably upstairs in their rooms, sir. We've told them to stay inside the hotel and we've taken their ID cards, phones and car keys so they can't get far.'

Marco nodded approvingly. 'I'm going to interview all three of them in the library a bit later on but first, I want to speak to Johnny Riccio. I imagine he's upstairs in the owner's private apartment.'

The constable went over to the reception desk and spoke to one of the receptionists. She nodded and picked up the phone. A short conversation ensued, after which the officer returned to where we were standing and addressed Marco again. 'He'll be right down. I'll wait by the lift and I'll bring him to you.'

Something occurred to me and I turned to the sergeant. 'Where did Riccio say he was this morning?'

'At a wine auction in Greve in Chianti.'

I thanked her and pulled out my phone to check a few things as we walked along the corridor and installed ourselves in the library, Marco and me behind the desk and Dini sitting at the end of it with her ever-present clipboard. We had to wait almost five minutes before a deferential tap at the door told us that the constable had located Johnny Riccio.

My reaction to seeing him for the first time was very similar to that of the sergeant. He was a tall, good-looking man with broad shoulders, olive skin and the blackest black hair imaginable. He was wearing a light-blue shirt that was so fresh, it still had the creases in it from where it had been folded. When he spotted Sergeant Dini, he flashed her a smile that highlighted his perfect teeth – a gift from a previous girlfriend maybe? – and I was impressed that she didn't recoil. She had definitely chosen the right adjective to describe him. He was decidedly creepy.

'Come in, Signor Riccio, and take a seat.' Marco was sounding polite, affable even, and the man nodded obligingly as he walked over to sit down.

'How can I help you, Inspector?' His eyes flicked briefly across my face before subjecting the sergeant to a leer that was probably intended to look alluring but which bore a remarkable similarity to the look Oscar gives his food when it's presented to him. Again, full marks to the sergeant. She didn't bat an eyelid.

'Signor Riccio, I wanted to inform you that we've been talking to the DIA about you.' From the way Riccio jumped, it was clear that he recognised the acronym but Marco pretended not to have noticed. 'That's the department of the Ministry of Justice specifically interested in the Mafia, whether Camorra, 'Ndrangheta, Cosa Nostra or the SCU.' Marco was still looking friendly, but a cloud had settled on Riccio's face. Still speaking gently, Marco continued. 'I imagine you're familiar with the SCU, the *Sacra Corona Unita*, from Puglia.'

I saw Riccio take a few deep breaths before unsuccessfully attempting an uninterested tone. 'Why should I know anything about the Mafia?'

'You tell me, but you do know about the SCU, don't you?'

'Only what I read in the papers. I thought they'd all been locked up.'

'Did you ever come across any of them back in your drug-dealing days?' Marco held up his hand to prevent an outburst from Riccio. 'Of course, I remember you told us that you're a reformed character now and I applaud that. I was just wondering what you know about these organisations.'

'Next to nothing. When I was dealing drugs, that was mostly in France, and the Italian Mafia doesn't extend across the border.'

Even Oscar at my feet probably knew how ridiculous that notion was. The Mafia, of whatever complexion, has tentacles across the world, and I had certainly come across mafiosi in London. Marco nodded as if in agreement before changing the subject.

'You said that you're a wine dealer. Tell me what you know about wine fraud; in particular, the way some unscrupulous producers mix good wine with less expensive wine so as to increase their profits at the expense of the buyer.'

Once again, I saw Riccio jump. It took him a moment or two to collect himself before replying. 'Wine fraud? Never heard of it.'

Marco gave him a pitying look. 'A wine trader who hasn't heard of fraud. What kind of trader are you?' He leant forward towards Riccio, his genial air now long gone. 'Or maybe you aren't a wine trader at all.'

'Of course I am, that's what I said.' The smooth-talking Latin lover was sounding decidedly flustered and I decided to increase the pressure on him.

'Signor Riccio, can you tell me where you went this morning?'

'I've been at a wine auction in Greve in Chianti. That's why I'm here in Tuscany. I've been visiting auctions and wine producers.'

'I wonder if you would tell us what sort of wine you bought this morning, please.'

Johnny Riccio looked at me in surprise. 'Chianti, of course. The clue's in the name: Greve in *Chianti*.' A hint of his earlier self-confidence returned – but it didn't last long as I continued.

'I'm particularly interested in where the wine auction this morning took place.' I gave him a long, hard look. 'I imagine it wasn't in the middle of the main square of Greve in Chianti.'

He was definitely struggling for an answer and even he must have realised that he was in a hole. I heaped on the pressure.

'Or maybe there wasn't a wine auction at all? I can't find any trace of an auction in Greve mentioned on the Internet.'

After a few seconds, he looked up, a sly expression on his face.

'Can I be sure that what I tell you remains private between us – sort of like confessing to a priest?'

Although I had a feeling that any priest who heard Riccio's confession would be in for a marathon session.

Marco replied in an even voice. 'It depends if it has any bearing on the case. If it's something private to you, then you have my word that it won't go any further.'

Riccio appeared reassured. 'Well, you see, it's like this, Inspector: I had an assignation this morning.'

Marco raised an eyebrow. 'A *romantic* assignation? You mean a date?'

Riccio nodded. 'I have a girlfriend in Florence and she wanted to see me.'

I glanced across at the sergeant and saw her roll her eyes. First Matthew White and now this character – what was it about some men? Digger's gut feeling that Riccio was unsuitable for his daughter had been more than vindicated. Marco asked him for contact details of the woman in question so he could verify the truth of what we'd been told and the sergeant made a note of the name and number as Marco resumed the questioning.

'So are you a wine merchant or aren't you?'

'Yes, I am, I buy and export wine in bulk.' Riccio allowed a self-deprecating look to appear on his face. 'But, to be honest, I don't normally deal with top-of-the-range wines. My contacts overseas are normally looking for wine that's above all cheap.'

'Does that include the wine from this winery?'

'Rockstar wine sells very well abroad. I'm their most important customer. I shift thousands of litres a year.'

'How long have you been aware that the manager of this winery has been mixing good Chianti with cheap imported wine?'

Riccio wasn't a talented actor. His reaction to the question was to drop his eyes and develop a sudden interest in his fingers. After a bit, he mumbled, 'I don't know anything about that.'

The hard edge was back in Marco's voice. 'Let me put it to you that not only did you know full well that the wine was substandard but you also actively collaborated with the manager to silence an investigative journalist who had discovered the fraud. Are you a murderer, Signor Riccio?'

Riccio looked up and shook his head. 'No, of course I'm not. I'm not a murderer. Besides, why would I want to murder a journalist? I'm not the person committing the fraud; I'm just a well-intentioned buyer of the product.' His voice strengthened a bit as he gained in confidence. 'I haven't done anything wrong, and you have no evidence that I did.'

And he was right about that.

22

THURSDAY EVENING

It was almost seven by the time Marco sent Johnny Riccio off with instructions not to leave the hotel. After the door closed behind him, Marco stood up and looked over towards the sergeant and me.

'I don't know about you two, but I could do with a coffee.'

We followed him through to the bar. A number of tables were occupied but I couldn't see any of the suspects. Through the windows, we could see the downpour continuing and broad puddles had formed on the ground outside. We chose a table at the far end of the room, away from prying ears, and ordered three coffees and a bowl of water.

Once the waitress had gone off, Marco turned the conversation to the interview with Johnny Riccio.

'Well, what do we think of Signor Riccio, Dini? Apart from him being creepy, what do you think are the chances that he's also a murderer?'

The sergeant replied straight away. 'It wouldn't surprise me in the slightest. When you mentioned the Mafia, there was an immediate reaction from him and the same applies to when you were talking about wine fraud. Maybe he's responsible for all four killings.'

'Dan, any thoughts?' Marco was tapping the end of his pencil on his notebook, clearly thinking deeply.

I, too, had been giving it a lot of thought. 'He has no alibi for the time of Greenbank's death on Tuesday afternoon, nor for lunchtime today. His alibi for the two killings overnight is that he was in bed with Florida but we know that he could have drugged her with Rohypnol and she wouldn't remember him leaving the room. So, as far as opportunity's concerned, he qualifies. As Sergeant Dini says, he's big, strong, and eminently capable of committing the murders, so there's no question that he had the means. That leaves us with trying to establish his motive and that's where it gets tricky.'

Marco nodded in agreement. 'In an ideal world, we would get a call any minute now from the *Antimafia* people in Rome telling us that he's known to them and suspicious. If that were the case, I'd say he could well be the perpetrator of all four murders. I'm going to get our people to investigate his background some more, particularly his bank records, in the hope of working out just exactly where all his money comes from. In the meantime, I'm keeping him firmly on my list of suspects.'

The waitress returned with our drinks and we sat there for a few minutes in silence – apart from slurping sounds from under the table as Oscar quenched his thirst. I had taken only an initial sip of my coffee when the door was flung open and one of the constables came rushing in, attracting curious – and uneasy – looks from the other guests. He ran over to our table and saluted. 'It's Davide Cassano. Somebody's tried to strangle him.'

We jumped to our feet and Marco was the first to react. '*Tried* to strangle him? Is he still alive?'

The constable nodded. 'Yes, the intruder was disturbed and

ran off. Cassano had the strength to call Reception and I've just been up there now. Constable Greco's mounting guard at Cassano's door.'

Marco glanced at me. 'You coming, Dan?'

'Just try and stop me.'

Abandoning our coffees, we ran along the corridor and up the stairs, Oscar charging up ahead of us joyfully. When we reached the second-floor landing, we turned left and were soon at room twenty-seven. An officer was waiting outside and he opened the door for us. Inside the room, we found Davide Cassano, the would-be Mafia boss, sitting on the bed dabbing his throat with a wet towel. There was a nasty red welt around his throat and he was breathing heavily. Marco and Dini went across to him while I stayed by the door with Oscar.

'Signor Cassano, are you all right?' Marco sounded concerned. 'Would you like us to call a doctor?'

Cassano looked up and, after a few moments' reflection, shook his head. 'No, I'm okay.'

Marco pulled up a chair and sat down in front of him. 'Do you feel up to telling us what happened?'

Cassano nodded. 'There was a knock at the door and I asked who it was. The answer came back, "Room Service", so I opened the door and was confronted by a man wearing a black balaclava and gloves. Before I could slam the door in his face, he pushed me backwards against one of the chairs and I tripped and fell. The next thing I knew, I was on my face, there was a knee in my back, there was something around my throat and he was trying to strangle me.' He stopped and took a few deep breaths.

'What did he have around your throat?'

Cassano pointed to the end of the bed where a blue and black striped tie was lying in a crumpled heap.

Marco nodded. 'So you were lying on the floor with the

aggressor on top of you, being choked to death with a tie, but then what happened?'

'I don't really know. There might have been a noise outside the room but it's hard to say. I was fighting for my life at the time. Anyway, whatever it was, I suddenly felt the pressure on my back and throat released and I turned in time to see him disappear out of the door. I crawled across to the phone, called Reception, and your officers appeared a minute later.'

'Who does the tie belong to? Is it yours?'

Cassano shook his head but Sergeant Dini cut in. 'I've seen it before, sir. When we were searching the other rooms, I saw it hanging in the wardrobe belonging to one of the bodyguards. I'm pretty sure it was Giuseppe Fosca's room – in fact, I know it was. I can visualise it hanging there.'

'Bag it and get it to Forensics. Even though the assailant was wearing gloves, there might be traces of DNA or other clues on it.'

I stood there and digested what I'd just heard. By the sound of it, Cassano had had a very narrow escape from death. If the tie turned out to belong to Fosca, what did that mean? Was he the would-be strangler or might this be yet another attempt to muddy the waters by the real killer? The only good news was that the main suspects had now whittled themselves down to just three: the two remaining bodyguards, Fosca and Torchio, or Johnny Riccio. Plus, of course, a hypothetical shadowy hitman sent from Puglia who had been able to hide his tracks perfectly so far.

'Can you give us a description of your aggressor?' Marco was studying the victim carefully. Cassano was still looking shaken, but unharmed apart from the marks on his throat and neck. 'You said his face was covered and he was wearing gloves, but did you notice anything else? What sort of clothes was he wearing? What did he smell like? Anything at all that might help us.'

I could see Cassano trying to concentrate. 'Smell? Nothing. As for his clothes, I think they were dark, like his gloves, but I really can't recall with any precision. It all happened so quickly. One minute, I was standing at the door and the next, I was face down on the floor with some guy trying to kill me.'

'Are you sure it was a man?'

He nodded decisively. 'No question. He was a man and a strong one at that. No woman could have done what he did to me.'

I wasn't so sure. I remembered a case back in the UK where a man had been seriously beaten up and left for dead by his former lover, a pint-sized woman who turned out to be an expert at Krav Maga, the brutal Israeli system of unarmed combat. Still, on balance, Cassano was probably right about his attacker having been a man.

'And can you think of any reason why you were assaulted? Three of your colleagues are dead. Are you sure you can't think of a reason why?'

Just like when we'd interviewed him earlier, he shook his head and gave a helpless shrug. 'How should I know? I reckon there's a maniac on the loose. Tomorrow, first thing, I'm out of here.'

After a few more tries, Marco finally gave up and we left Cassano with his wet towel and his whisky bottle, now barely a quarter full. Outside in the corridor, Marco stopped and looked at Dini and me. 'Right, Dini, we need to interview Fosca and Torchio as well as Johnny Riccio all over again. Let's see which of them can produce a credible alibi. Dan, you go on home. Thanks again for all the help. I'm sorry I ruined Anna's birthday celebrations.'

'It was fine, Marco. Don't worry about it. I've enjoyed myself.' And I had. Once a murder squad detective, always a murder squad detective. But now I had another more pressing priority. I wished them good hunting and headed for the stairs.

Outside the front door, it was still bucketing with rain and Oscar and I were both drenched by the time we reached the van. I opened the back door, he leapt in, and I slammed it again before running for the driver's door. No sooner had I sat down than I heard the unmistakable sound of Oscar shaking himself and a cloud of Labrador-scented water coated the inside of the van and landed on the back of my head.

By the time I had navigated my way home through appalling driving conditions, splashing through streams flooding across the roads and through puddles deep enough to have me worrying that I might end up stuck, I had almost dried out, but the Labrador odour persisted. This was made clear to me by Anna as I walked in the door. She breathed in, grimaced and pointed towards the stairs.

'I'll do my best to dry Oscar while you go and change.' She shot me a little grin. 'And a shower would probably be a good idea too.'

By the time I came back downstairs again, I felt refreshed and I found Oscar rolling about on the floor, tail wagging happily, as Anna shoved his old towel into the washing machine. She looked up, smiled, and held out her arms towards me. 'That's better! Now come over and say hello properly.'

'Just one moment.' I went to the fridge and took out the bottle of real French champagne that I'd put in there in readiness for this evening. I opened the bottle and filled two glasses before going across to where she was standing. 'Here, *buon anniversario*.' I kissed her softly and handed her a glass. 'Cheers, Anna, and happy birthday. You're the best thing that's happened to me for years.' A movement at my feet and a nudge of a nose reminded me of my other recent asset. I had had Oscar now for two years and I couldn't imagine life without him. I scratched his nose and he grunted happily.

Neither of us – excluding Oscar – felt like a big meal after our excellent lunch so we just had some cheese and fresh figs, followed by home-made meringue ice cream from Leonardo's ice-cream shop in Montevolpone. At nine-thirty, I looked out of the door and saw that the rain had stopped – at least for now – so I took Oscar out for a last walk, while Anna went upstairs to bed. Although I tried to keep him on the white gravel track, he inevitably disappeared into the vines and olive trees from time to time and returned soaking wet and looking like something that had crawled out of a swamp. It took me twenty minutes when I got back home to wash him and dry him before he settled in his basket and I finally made my way up to the bedroom. The only light in the room came from the little bedside light and Anna was already in bed, waiting for me. I headed for the bathroom and was just coming out to join her when my phone started ringing. I picked it off the bedside table, gave her an apologetic smile, and answered it automatically without checking the caller ID.

'*Pronto.*'

'Dan, hi, I just wanted to tell you that I'm back home.' It was Helen. Silently cursing that she'd chosen to call rather than send a text, I lowered my voice and answered.

'Oh, that's good. Thank you for letting me know.' I was about to press the off button when she carried on.

'It was so good to see you again, Dan. I can't thank you enough for helping me after I made such a fool of myself.'

'Don't worry about it. You weren't to know that White was such a pain.'

'I know this much. You would never have treated me the way he did.'

By this time, I was desperate for the call to end so I hastily invented an excuse. 'Well, thanks for letting me know you're home. I have to go. I'm waiting for a call from the police.'

I realised my mistake as I said it, but it was too late. 'Have you caught the murderer?' She sounded fascinated. 'Who was it?'

I glanced across at Anna, who had turned her head away and pulled the sheet over her face. 'As far as I know, the police are still investigating, although I get the feeling they're closing in on the perpetrator.'

'What about you? Are you still investigating as well?'

'No, I was just helping out with the language.'

'Don't give me that. I know you all too well. I bet you're hard at it now.'

Involuntarily, I glanced across at the figure under the sheet. Chance would be a fine thing. 'No, to be honest, I was about to go to bed.'

Finally, she got the message. 'Well, I won't keep you but I just wanted to say a big thank you yet again. You're a good man, Dan.' There was the unmistakable sound of a kiss and then, at long last, she rang off.

I dropped my phone back onto the bedside table and slipped into bed, where I snuggled up to Anna and whispered into her ear. 'That was Helen. She's home. That'll be the last I hear from her... honest.'

I got no answer.

23

FRIDAY EARLY MORNING

I slept badly and got up at seven, tiptoeing about so as not to wake Anna. Downstairs, I found Oscar looking bouncy and he barked excitedly as he saw me head for the door.

'Oscar, shush!' I hissed at him sotto voce. 'Anna's still asleep.' In return, I got a slobbery lick, but he did at least shut up.

Outside, I could see that it had rained some more during the night as there were puddles at the edge of the parking area a couple of inches deep and the sky was still an ominous dark-grey colour. Oscar splashed about happily before heading into the nearby field, from which he returned looking like a chocolate Labrador. Given that he was now coated in mud, I headed down through the rough scrub of a patch of no man's land to the little stream to give him a chance to go for a swim and clean himself up. As a result of the rain, the little pool where he normally splashed about had disappeared beneath a broad sheet of fast-moving water, pouring off the hillside. I kept a close eye on him as he leapt joyously in and swam about, barking at me to throw him a stick to retrieve, and I was relieved to see that he wasn't washed away. The last thing I felt like doing was having to dive into the river to rescue him.

While we played, my mind returned to the anticlimactic way Anna's birthday celebrations had finished. I had tried several times to get her to talk to me in bed but without success, and in the end, all I'd been able to do was to roll over and try to get to sleep. What had stopped me from drifting off easily was that I had found myself feeling conflicted. On the one hand, I could understand Anna's insecurity at my ex-wife's sudden reappearance in my life. On the other hand, there was my frustration that Anna hadn't been prepared to accept my word that there was no longer anything between me and Helen and there never would be. Anna had never spoken to me about the reasons why she and her husband of twenty years had divorced, and I'd never asked her. Had he maybe left her for another woman and it was the memory of that betrayal that was affecting her now? Alternatively, was I to blame? Should I have walked away from the investigation as soon as Helen appeared on the scene or, at least, should I have been much more distant towards her? Was this all my fault? As I watched Oscar struggling to swim against the current, I knew how he felt.

We were out for over half an hour and when we got back to the house, the first thing I noticed was that Anna's car was no longer parked outside. She had gone. I went inside and checked to see if she'd left me a note and was relieved to see a piece of paper on the kitchen table. It couldn't exactly be described as a billet-doux.

Gone to work

Nothing more than that. As I set about drying my soaking-wet dog, I tried discussing the conundrum with him but without any more response than an occasional lick. To cheer myself up, I made a fry-up of bacon and a couple of eggs. I don't often have a cooked breakfast but I felt I needed the boost today, and Oscar at my side made short work of the bacon rind as always.

After a shower and a change of clothes, I felt a bit better and was getting ready to go into the office for the first time in days when my phone started ringing. I picked it up eagerly but it wasn't Anna calling. Instead, it was Virgilio.

'*Ciao*, Dan, good night last night?'

'It was certainly a wet one.' I decided not to tell him the truth of how the evening had ended. 'Any news your end?'

'Brilliant news.' I could hear the enthusiasm in his voice. 'Remind me to send a case of good wine to a very helpful guy called Inspector Dufour of the Carcassonne police. They've broken all speed records and have identified the haulage firm and the wine tanker. Unfortunately, they haven't been able to interview the driver yet as he's in the Netherlands with a delivery and won't be back until this evening, but they've already swabbed the cab of the truck and they've sent us the results. Would you believe that one of the DNA samples they've identified inside the cab of the truck is a perfect match with one of our suspects? Want to hazard a guess who?'

'The obvious culprit is Mancini. Am I right?'

'I'm pretty sure he was involved, but the DNA from the truck isn't his. It belongs to Johnny Riccio.'

'Well, well, well. Do you think he's also responsible for the murders at the hotel? By the way, when I left yesterday afternoon, Marco was going to interview the two remaining bodyguards. What did Fosca say about his tie being used to strangle Cassano?'

'What do you think? He claimed to be amazed and he told us he had no idea how it had got there. DNA tests on the tie reveal only two people – Fosca and Cassano himself – but he did say his attacker was wearing gloves. As for Riccio, of course he had free run of the place, so he was ideally positioned to carry out the killings, but we still need a motive.'

'Any word back from *Antimafia*?'

'Remarkably yes, at seven-thirty this morning. The bad news is that Riccio isn't on their radar and neither is Mancini.'

'So that makes it less likely, though not impossible, that he's a Mafia hitman. I can see him being involved in the first murder. He told us he's the winery's biggest customer and it wouldn't surprise me in the slightest if he and Mancini were working together to defraud Digger – and the wine-buying public. What I can't understand is what possible connection he might have had with any of the people who died at the hotel. Are you going to pick him up?'

'Marco's on his way now. He'll bring him to the *questura* and we'll question him there. I was wondering, seeing as you've been involved with the case, whether you'd like to be in on the questioning.'

The answer to that one was yes but, first, I knew I needed to speak to Anna. I thanked him for the offer and told him I had to go into the office first, but if I could, I'd come across and join them. As soon as the call ended, I picked up my keys and looked across at Oscar, who was lying stretched out on the floor near the door with one eye open.

'Fancy a trip to Florence?'

In response, he jumped to his feet and we hurried out to the van. It was very soggy outside, and the sky was still dark grey. There was a lot of surface water about and I was glad I was going downhill, rather than trying to slip and slide my way up the muddy track. Hopefully, by the time I got home again tonight, it would have dried out a bit, although the clouds looked menacing.

It took me over half an hour to get into Florence through the morning traffic and I pulled in through the archway to the court-yard below my office at just before nine.

Dan Armstrong Investigations occupies a small apartment in a magnificent sixteenth-century building situated just inside the *centro storico*. The courtyard walls still have iron rings set in them for tethering horses, and grooves in the flagstones show where carriage wheels used to pass. Although I'd been working here for months now, a fascinating sense of history still spread through me every time I came here. Today, though, I had other things on my mind. Oscar and I ran up the stairs to the office where I found Lina, sitting at her desk. She had been working with me now for almost six months and she had made my life a lot easier as a result. She had also developed a close friendship with Anna and it was this that interested me in particular this morning. I went over and shook her left hand while her right hand was busy fending off a boisterous welcome from Oscar.

'*Ciao*, Lina. I need your advice.'

She didn't look surprised. 'I think I know what this is all about. I've just been talking to Anna.'

'Ah, right. What did she tell you?'

'That she thinks your ex-wife might be making a play for you again. Is that what you want my advice about?'

'Absolutely. You see, I had a completely chance meeting with Helen and I'm afraid Anna's worried that I'm about to go off and leave her.'

Lina smiled sympathetically. 'And you aren't?'

'Of course not. Meeting Helen again brought back a lot of memories, and not all of them were good. In fact, if I needed convincing that things between me and Helen were all over – which I don't – these past two days have definitely made that crystal clear.'

'From what Anna told me just now, she has a feeling your ex-wife doesn't feel the same way.'

'I'm not so sure, but even if she is thinking of getting back together, I'm with Anna now and that's that.'

'That's good to hear. Have you told Anna that?'

'I thought I had and I thought everything was sorted between us, but then I got a phone call from Helen last night to tell me that she'd got back to the UK safely and although I tried explaining to Anna, I got no response, and she left home before I came back from my early-morning walk with Oscar so I couldn't speak to her again.' The words came tumbling out in a jumbled mess and I saw Oscar turn and stare at me in bemusement.

Lina smiled at me again. 'And now you want my advice?' I nodded mutely and she carried on, the smile still on her face. 'You already said it yourself. You need to talk to her. From what she told me, she's working in her office this morning. There's nothing urgent in your diary here so why don't you head over there now and speak to her?'

'You think she'll listen to me?' I could hear myself sounding remarkably clueless.

'I know she will. Go on, go and see her now. It's only a ten-minute walk, after all.'

* * *

Florence University's department of Medieval and Renaissance Studies is situated inside a wonderful, faded ochre-coloured building not far from the Duomo. The corridor leading to Anna's office is paved with a charming and complex pattern of grey and white ceramic tiles and the high ceiling is made up of a series of elegant arches. For somebody with an interest in history, it's a fascinating place, but this morning, I barely noticed my beautiful surroundings as I hurried along to her door. I stopped outside, took a deep breath, and was about to tap on the door when it opened and a student with his hair tied up in a knot came out with a sheaf of papers in his hand. Behind him, sitting at her desk, I could see Anna. As she made eye contact with me, I gave her a little wave.

'Can I come in?'

She beckoned with her hand and I went in, closing the door behind me. Oscar immediately charged over to say hello – and to get close to the drawer where she keeps biscuits for him – while I took my time, doing my best to compose my thoughts.

'*Ciao*, Anna. I need to talk to you.'

She indicated a wooden chair in front of her desk and I sat down, feeling like a naughty schoolboy being called up in front of the head. While Oscar leant against her and she stroked his ears, I launched into my explanation. In the end, it wasn't that complicated.

'I'm sorry I missed you this morning, but there's something you need to know.' I could see her following my words closely and the expression on her face was not so much disapproving as nervous, and I hastened to reassure her. 'You need to know that you're the only woman in my life – apart from Tricia and my mum – and that's the way I always want it to be. Please believe me when I tell you that I heaved a massive sigh of relief when I said goodbye to Helen at the airport yesterday. She's the past, Anna, and you're the present and, if you'll have me, the future.'

I sat there in silence for a few moments before she responded, a softer expression appearing on her face. 'Thank you, Dan, but *I* need to apologise to you. I suppose it was just the shock of seeing you with your ex-wife that upset me, and I've been behaving like a jealous teenager. Just like you, I think we have something really special and I want you to be in my future as well.'

I felt a massive weight lifted off my shoulders and I glanced across the desk at her. 'Would I be infringing university regulations if I came around to your side of the desk and gave you a kiss?'

She was smiling now. 'I'll be disappointed if you don't. I'm sorry I behaved like an idiot.'

I smiled back at her as I stood up. 'I'm the expert around here at behaving like an idiot. We're made for each other.'

24

FRIDAY MORNING

I got to the *questura* at just after nine-thirty, feeling a lot happier. So was Oscar, but that was as a result of having been handed a big, bone-shaped biscuit from Anna's special drawer. I found Virgilio, Marco and the sergeant also looking happy, but for a different reason. Marco greeted me with the news.

'Giovanni "Johnny" Riccio is sitting in an interview room stewing, but we've just finished talking to Mancini. He started out monosyllabic, but when we told him we'd arrested Riccio and that we had incontrovertible proof that it had been Riccio who'd driven the truck over Greenbank's body, the floodgates suddenly opened. The way Mancini tells the story, he's just a helpless pawn and the real bad guy is Riccio.' He grinned at me. 'But he would say that, wouldn't he? He told us the idea for mixing good wine with cheap wine came from Riccio a couple of years ago. Apparently, Riccio told him he works with half a dozen other producers who do the exact same thing with him.'

'Big business!' I was impressed. 'Does this mean that Greenbank came to Tuscany to investigate wine fraud, and it was nothing to do with the Mafia?'

'It certainly looks that way. Mancini flatly denies that he or Riccio have anything to do with organised crime – apart from their own criminal undertaking at the winery.'

'And who killed Greenbank? Let me guess: Mancini swears on his mother's grave that it was Riccio, right?'

'Dead right and I'm prepared to bet my *tredicesima* that when we speak to Riccio, he'll say it was Mancini.'

I smiled. Most Italians get a thirteenth month's pay at Christmas, the *tredicesima*, but I felt sure that in this case, Marco could bet his house and his car as well and still come out a winner. I'd seen it so many times in my career – when the chips are down, the rats in the trap so often turn upon each other. 'Whichever of them did it, at least we now have somebody prepared to admit that the murder was committed there.'

Virgilio gave a contented smile. 'Exactly. According to Mancini, Riccio told him he'd heard that they had a journalist on their heels and he sent him messages, trying to frighten him off. When that didn't work, he made sure he kept an eye out for him. When he spotted Greenbank, he strangled him with a piece of rope and pulled him into the cantina to do it undisturbed. This chimes with what White told us. We've got a team going through the cantina millimetre by millimetre as we speak, looking specifically for the murder weapon. Hopefully, they'll find it and we'll be able to get the perpetrator's DNA off it.'

I clapped the three of them on the back. 'Well done, that's one murder solved. What about the three at the hotel? I imagine Mancini continues to disclaim any knowledge of those guys.'

Marco nodded. 'And I tended to believe him.' His satisfied air left him. 'So, of course, that leaves us high and dry. You never know, it could be that Riccio's our man for all four murders but, if not, we're back to the two remaining bodyguards and Cassano, although his recent narrow escape from being strangled would tend to put him in the clear.'

Virgilio was also looking less elated now. 'I'm with you, Marco. I certainly don't think Mancini had anything to do with those deaths. Either Torchio or Fosca or both of them have to be hitmen, sent to wipe out the plotters. Let's see what Johnny Riccio has to say for himself and, if not, then it's back to the hotel one more time. Presumably, all three are still there?'

'Yes, Cassano was making noises yesterday about wanting to get away first thing this morning, but I've given all three of them instructions to stay put. The fact that we've also got their documents and car keys should mean that they aren't going anywhere fast.' Marco looked across at me. 'Do you want to sit in on the interview with Riccio or would you prefer to watch through the mirror?'

'Thanks for the invitation, but I'm more than happy to get myself a cup of coffee and sit and watch from behind the glass. It's always good to see professionals at work.'

Marco gave me a friendly punch on the shoulder and turned to the sergeant. 'Dini, why don't you get a coffee for yourself and one for Dan and you can both watch proceedings from the observation room?'

She nodded and raised an eyebrow in my direction. I mouthed the word 'cappuccino' and she headed off, while I followed Marco and Virgilio down the corridor to the room next to the interview room. I went in and took a seat facing the two-way mirror, through which I could see the two officers sitting down opposite Johnny Riccio with a large custody officer standing impassively in the background. Sergeant Dini arrived alongside me a minute later with the coffees, pressed the Listen switch on the panel on the wall, and Marco's voice flooded in.

'...and you are resident in Paris?'

'Yes.' Riccio was looking and sounding downbeat, but maybe there was also an element of trepidation in him this time as well.

'You were born in Treviso, you hold an Italian passport, and you claim to be a wine merchant?'

'Yes.'

'How long have you known Fabiano Mancini from the Rockstar winery?'

'About three years.' Still sounding sullen.

'It might interest you to know that he has now admitted wine fraud and he's told us that you suggested the idea to him. What do you have to say to that accusation?'

Riccio's face paled, but I could see that he was still trying to fight his corner. 'The man's a liar. I assume he's lying to save his own skin. I don't deal in substandard wine.'

'But that's not all. He claims that on Tuesday afternoon, you murdered a British journalist called Anthony Greenbank. How do you respond to that?'

'I already told you: I'm no murderer.' There was even a bit of his former bluster in his voice now, but it didn't last long.

'Tell me, then, Signor Riccio, how it is that your DNA's been found on the steering wheel of a French-registered truck that came to the winery to deliver wine that day.'

Even over the intercom, I distinctly heard Riccio gulp. 'There must be some mistake.' He was struggling for words, and Virgilio added a bit of weight to the interrogation with a little white lie.

'The French police have been very helpful and they've interviewed the driver of that truck. He confirms that you not only sat in the driving seat but you drove it over the lifeless body of the journalist in the hope of making his death look like a hit-and-run accident.' He waited a few seconds to heighten the dramatic tension before continuing. 'In the light of this information, would you like to modify your previous statement? It seems quite clear to us, Signor Riccio, that you're a killer, and a cold-blooded one at that.'

There was a pregnant pause, during which I could almost see the man's brain working, desperately looking for a way out. Finally, he must have realised that there was no escape and what he said next would have justified Marco betting his life savings.

'All right, so I drove the truck over the body, but the guy was already dead. Mancini killed him. He strangled him. I saw it happen and tried to stop him, but it was no use.'

Marco looked direct at me through the mirror and winked before taking up the questioning again, doing his best to get the suspect to admit involvement in the murders at the hotel but without success. Finally, he and Virgilio gave up and instructed the custody officer to take Riccio to the cells, after which Dini and I finished our coffees and went through to the interview room. After mutual congratulations, Marco announced his next steps.

'I'm on my way to the hotel now to interview the two remaining bodyguards. I'm convinced the murderer of Bellomo, Calabrese and Rossini has to be one of them – or maybe even both of them.'

I left it to Virgilio to ask the inevitable question. 'So what happens if they both continue to plead innocence? Do we have any substantial evidence? At the moment, all we have is the Rohypnol in Torchio's cistern and I think we're all agreed that this was almost certainly planted there. The only DNA on the tie used to strangle Cassano belongs to the owner, Fosca, and Cassano himself from when he loosened it off, so nothing new there. Whoever the murderer is, he's a pro.'

Marco looked equally dubious. 'On that basis, I suppose the more likely perpetrator is Fosca, but I must admit that Arturo

Torchio struck me as a dangerous character. What do you think, Dan?'

'I agree with you that Torchio also struck me as the most potentially murderous of the bodyguards. If we assume for a moment that he's a professional killer and one who has successfully managed to avoid your *Antimafia* people, then I wouldn't put it past him to have deliberately put the Rohypnol in his own cistern so as to steer our attention away from himself. First of all, he tried the same trick with the pair of shoes in White's waste bin in the hope of incriminating White, but when that didn't work, he tried something a bit more subtle, finishing up with the attempted murder of Cassano with Fosca's tie.'

Virgilio nodded. 'And talking of trying again, that attempt on Cassano's life very nearly succeeded. We need to either find our murderer or, at the very least, make sure that Torchio, Fosca and Cassano go their separate ways as quickly as possible. We don't want another murder on our hands and I'm sure the hotel doesn't either – let alone the public prosecutor, who's going crazy. Keeping these guys in their rooms side by side is an accident – or rather a murder – waiting to happen.' He stood up. 'I'll come with you, Marco. You interview one bodyguard and I'll speak to the other and if they continue to stonewall, I don't think we'll have any option but to let them go.' I could hear the disappointment in his voice. 'Come on, the sooner we start, the sooner we finish.'

I wished them well. 'At least you've got Greenbank's killers locked up. That's a start.'

We shook hands and Oscar and I walked back through the crowded streets to my office. When I got there, Lina told me there was nothing pressing in the diary so, reluctantly, I sat down and opened my laptop. The online Forensic Cyber Security course beckoned.

I'd been studying hard for barely twenty minutes when something I read struck a chord with me. I was reading about a notorious Hungarian hacker who had deliberately hacked his own computer in an attempt to direct police attention away from himself by appearing to be a victim. It had almost worked and, had it not been for one simple oversight by him, he might well have got away with it. The chapter heading of this particular module was 'Misdirection' and a sudden thought occurred to me.

Just as Torchio might well have deliberately planted the Rohypnol in his toilet in an attempt to direct suspicion away from himself, the same could maybe apply to Cassano, the last man standing of the three would-be Mafia bosses. What if he had deliberately taken Fosca's tie so as to incriminate *him* and used it to strangle himself? Or, rather, to simulate strangulation. I thought back to the scene in his suite the previous day. There had been an angry red mark around his neck and throat, but there had been no sign of blood. In my experience, the natural reaction of anybody being strangled is to grip the rope or wire and desperately try to pull it away or loosen it. In so doing, the victim's throat almost always ends up with scratch marks inflicted by his or her own fingernails in a desperate attempt to escape. I had noted no scratches on Cassano's throat. Maybe we'd been too quick to dismiss him from the list of prime suspects.

I picked up my phone and tried calling first Marco, then Virgilio, and then Sergeant Dini but without success. Presumably, they were interviewing the suspects. After a few moments' thought, I decided to go to the Podere dei Santi myself. This was partly so I could communicate with the police officers but, if I was honest, it was also because I rather fancied being in at the death if Cassano did indeed turn out to be a multiple murderer.

25

FRIDAY MID-MORNING

It took over three quarters of an hour to get to the hotel, not because of the traffic but because of the surface water lying on the roads. A huge, black cloud had rolled up and it started raining again as I left the outskirts of Florence and by the time I got into the open country, it was once again tipping it down. Even with the wipers on the fastest setting, it was like driving through fog. When I got onto the more minor roads leading south into the hills, I found myself having to skirt around huge puddles, some extending right across the road and one, in particular, that looked seriously deep and blocked the way completely. To avoid it, I had to reverse, turn onto a rough gravel track and take a loop around above the flood before rejoining the road by a little road-side café where the owner was busy brushing muddy water out of the entrance. Clearly, the fresh downpour on top of the overnight rain had flooded his premises.

As I picked my way towards the hotel, I tried calling Virgilio again and this time, he answered.

'*Pronto.*'

'*Ciao*, Virgilio. Listen, I've had a thought. Have you seen Cassano this morning?'

'Not yet. He's next on our list of interviewees. Absolutely no joy from either of the bodyguards. Why do you ask?'

'All the way through this case, we've been faced with disinformation. There were the trainers in the waste bin, the Rohypnol in the toilet, Fosca's tie around Cassano's neck; all designed to muddy the waters. It's just occurred to me that Cassano's near-death experience yesterday might have been more of the same. Go and examine the red mark on his neck more closely. I've a feeling he did it to himself. I have a very strong feeling that Cassano is the killer.'

'*Porca miseria*, you could be right. We'll get right on it. Thanks, Dan.'

'Here's hoping. By the way, I'm almost at the hotel. I thought I'd come out in person. See you in five minutes.'

It was closer to ten minutes of slow manoeuvring, my speed little more than walking pace at times as I fought my way through a wall of water, before I spotted the hotel in the distance. At that moment, my phone started ringing again. It was Marco and he sounded out of breath.

'All hell's broken loose here. Cassano's got away. He knocked one of our officers out and made a break for it. Downstairs, he was approached by Dini and a fight took place. Cassano's got hold of a knife and Dini's been stabbed but she fired at him and, from the bloodstains, Cassano's wounded too. He's disappeared into the vineyard so watch yourself. I've called for backup and dog handlers so he shouldn't be able to get away.'

'What a mess! How's Dini? Is she going to be okay?'

'She's lost a lot of blood, but she's conscious. She's tough, that one.' In spite of the gravity of the situation, I could hear respect in his voice.

As I made my way up the drive between the cypress trees towards the hotel, I scanned the vines on both sides closely, looking for any sign of Cassano, but all I could see through the curtain of torrential rain was greenery and thick, viscous mud. I pulled into the car park and jumped out to release Oscar from the boot. Sensibly, he immediately set off for the main entrance and shelter from the downpour. I was about to follow him when I heard a voice at my ear and felt a sharp point press against the side of my throat, perilously close to my carotid artery.

'Get back in the van.' It was Cassano and he sounded highly stressed. I felt a trickle of warm blood run down the side of my throat and wondered if it was coming from him or me. I looked around desperately but there was nobody else to be seen. The rain was now coming down even more heavily and the hotel entrance was barely visible. I turned to open the boot to let Oscar back in, but the voice at my ear became more urgent. 'Leave the dog. Get in.'

He sounded close to breaking point, and I could feel the hand holding the blade against my skin shaking. This was no time for heroics, so I headed for the driver's door slowly and carefully. When I reached it, I risked a question. 'Do you want to drive? The keys are in my pocket.'

'You drive; I can't.' I managed to glance down and saw a stream of blood running from the bottom of his trouser leg.

I opened the door and climbed into the driver's seat. I heard the door behind me slide open and then slam shut. A second later, the knife was once again at my throat.

'Drive.' His voice rose in pitch. 'I said drive, go!'

I attached my seat belt, started the engine, and set off. A glance in my rear-view mirror showed me the forlorn figure of a very wet black Labrador standing on the top step by the hotel entrance, staring pathetically at my tail lights. He would be all right, I told myself. At least he wasn't in a vehicle with a desperate murderer. I had been in tough situations before but, even so, I could feel my heart pounding like a steam train and I had to draw on all my years of experience to stop my hands from shaking. When we reached the bottom of the drive, I tried to turn my head towards him but the point of the knife against my throat stopped me.

'Which way? Left or right? Where are we going?'

'Right, towards Florence.' His voice sounded weaker, and I began to hope he might pass out soon from loss of blood.

I turned right and began to go back the way I'd come. Visibility through the downpour was appalling and the pools of water on the road had grown even deeper. I slowed to pick my way around them but the knife at my throat became more insistent and I heard Cassano shout in my ear. 'Faster, you imbecile. Faster!'

I did as instructed, desperately hoping that I wouldn't run into somebody coming the other way with no lights on. As I splashed through the puddles, walls of water sprayed up on both sides of me and it was at that point that an idea began to formulate in my mind. I was wearing a seat belt but quite obviously my passenger wasn't. Maybe if I could make the van stop very suddenly, he might be thrown off balance and I could make my escape. I did my best not to let my mind dwell on the possibility that the impact might result in the knife being stabbed into my artery and instead, I concentrated on the mechanics of the problem. The brakes on this relatively new vehicle worked very well, but what I really needed was a sudden impact. I was even considering ramming one of the cypresses at the roadside when it occurred to me that deep water would do just as well. At that moment, I spotted the roadside café and I knew that around the next bend I would find the road blocked by a flood. Taking a deep breath, I stamped my right foot to the floor and accelerated into the downpour, virtually blind to what was going on outside. I sensed rather than saw the road curve to the left and then we hit the floodwater and stopped dead.

I was thrown forward against my seat belt and simultaneously, there was a detonation and two airbags opened in front of my face, scratching my cheeks and totally blinding me for a few seconds. There was a heavy thud from behind me as Cassano made contact with the back of my seat or headrest and mercifully, the sharp point of the knife at my throat disappeared. Acting on instinct, I unclipped my seat belt and fought my way out of the folds of the constricting rubber airbags as they deflated. I tore the driver's door open, rolled out sideways and landed in two or three feet of remarkably cold, muddy water, but I didn't mind. I was alive and I could surely outrun a man with a bullet in his leg. I splashed over to the side, climbed out of the water and perched on an old milestone marked with the road number and 'Firenze 21 km'. I felt like an ancient mariner reaching shore after a shipwreck.

The rain was still pouring down without let-up, but it didn't matter to me. I vaguely noticed that the front of my shirt was turning pink and I reached up to feel my throat. When I removed my hand, my fingers were red with blood and this shook me for a moment. I pulled myself together and told myself that the wound didn't appear to be bleeding too badly. Certainly, there was no question of my carotid artery having been severed or I would be lying face down in the flood by now. I searched in my pockets for a tissue but there was nothing in there but waterlogged pulp. All I could do was to pull up my shirt and use the hem to press against the cut. When I gingerly removed it again, I was relieved to feel that the flow had definitely slowed.

I sat there and breathed deeply, gradually feeling my racing

heart slow to something approaching normal. My brain started
working again and I remembered that Marco had told me he'd
called for backup. Hopefully, this meant that in a short while,
police reinforcements would come up this very same road and
they could look after my erstwhile captor. There was no movement from the van and it looked as though Cassano had been
knocked out or otherwise incapacitated. Thought of him roused
me from my catatonic state.

I stood up and made my way back into the water again and
over to the van. There was no sign of Cassano, and for one
horrible moment, I thought he'd escaped, but when I got closer
and peered in through the side window, I saw his body slumped
across the back seat, immobile. I was just wondering whether I
should try to get him out and see if he could be resuscitated
when the sound of a siren attracted my attention. To my surprise,
the noise was coming from behind me, not from the direction of
Florence. Sure enough, a few seconds later, a police car skidded
to a halt just short of the water. The doors were flung open and
three figures appeared: Marco, Virgilio, and a big, black
Labrador.

Oscar spotted me immediately, leapt into the flood and
doggy-paddled towards me while Marco waded across behind
him. He looked absolutely soaked and it occurred to me that he
had probably had my very wet dog on his lap. When Oscar
reached me, he was whining joyfully and he almost drowned
himself in his attempts to climb into my arms. Moments later,
Marco got to me.

'Ciao, Dan. Are you all right?' I could see his eyes on my
throat and I was quick to reassure him – and me.

'Just a nick.' I did my best to sound more positive than I felt.
'I'll be fine. Cassano's in the van. He appears to be unconscious

but he might even be dead. He was bleeding very heavily from one leg or foot.'

'Dini said she hit him in the leg. I'll take a look at him.'

I left him to investigate the van and I waded across to where Virgilio was standing by the police car, his hair and clothes drenched by the downpour.

'*Ciao*, Virgilio.' I had to raise my voice to make myself heard over the drumming of the rain against the roof of the car.

He grabbed me by the shoulders and gave me a bearhug. '*Ciao*, Dan, I'm glad you're okay.' He stepped back and studied my throat. 'You're a lucky man. Just a flesh wound.'

'Thanks, I'm sure it's nothing serious. How's Dini?'

'Fortunately, there's a doctor among the guests and he's looking after her. He reckons she should pull through.'

'Thank God for that.' Now that he was on relatively dry land again. Oscar was up on his hind legs, pawing at me and making happy canine noises, his tail wagging furiously. I stroked his face in my hands and glanced across at Virgilio. 'How did you know I'd come down here with Cassano? I couldn't see anybody when we drove off.'

His face cracked into a grin. 'Your four-legged friend told us. He came charging into the hotel, soaking everybody, and started barking furiously until I followed him outside. There was no sign of you or the van, so I put two and two together. As partners go, you couldn't ask for better.'

I looked down into Oscar's big, brown eyes. 'Thanks, buddy. There's a steak with your name on it in the fridge back home.'

I swear he nodded his head and grinned at me.

At that moment, the sound of sirens approaching from the direction of Florence attracted our attention, and we looked up as a small convoy of police vehicles and a pair of ambulances appeared through the rain, stopping just in time to avoid the flood. I waded across to them with Oscar swimming happily alongside me. When I reached the other side, I pointed out the track a hundred yards back that would allow them to avoid the flood and get up to the hotel so the paramedics could look after Sergeant Dini.

Marco called across from the door of my van to one of the officers who had emerged from the first of the police cars. 'Lucchese, get Dan to the ambulance and make sure they patch him up. Cassano's alive but his leg's still bleeding. Leave one ambulance here and send the other one up to the hotel as fast as possible.' He turned his attention towards me again. 'The paramedics can clean you up while they sort Cassano out. Go on, you're making a terrible mess of your shirt and Anna won't be happy if you ruin it.'

26

FRIDAY LUNCHTIME

Things happened remarkably quickly after that. The paramedics cleaned and dressed the wound in my neck, remarking on how lucky I'd been. They told me the cut was less than a centimetre from the main artery and pointed out that if that had been sliced, I wouldn't be sitting there now. I thanked them for the information and did my best to relegate that to the more remote areas of my brain. It would probably resurface in a nightmare some time in the middle of the night but, for now, I just felt a great sense of relief. The good news – apart from my still being alive – was that while I was in the ambulance, the rain stopped as swiftly as it had begun. We all heard the exact moment it stopped. One minute, we were being almost deafened by the roar of the water on the roof of the ambulance and seconds later, there was blissful silence. It was as if the tap had been turned off again.

Sporting a clean, white, surgical dressing on my neck, I waded back through the floodwater with Oscar while the paramedics busied themselves with a very groggy Davide Cassano, the would-be boss of a renewed SCU, who would have lots of time to consider how things had gone wrong over the next decades in prison. I climbed into the car with Marco and Virgilio and we returned to the hotel. The staff at the reception desk were amazing. Taking one look at the three of us – plus a very wet Labrador – they allocated us one of the bedrooms, where we were able to strip off and do our best to wring as much water out of our clothes as possible before putting them back on. A young chambermaid brought us a heap of fresh towels and told me it was okay to use one of them to dry Oscar as well. She must have noted my bloodstained shirt and I was particularly impressed a few minutes later when there was a tap on the door and she reappeared with a fresh, white polo shirt for me – with the manager's compliments. It had 'Rockstar Chianti' embroidered on the left breast, but I didn't mind. I was going to wear it, not drink it, and it had the great attraction of being dry.

We went back downstairs again to find that the convoy from Florence had got around the flood, and Sergeant Dini was already in the ambulance speeding towards Florence. The uniformed sergeant gave me the news that they had very kindly towed my van out of the floodwater. I checked the time and saw that it was barely eleven-thirty. So much seemed to have happened this morning already. It occurred to me that I was supposed to be meeting Anna in Florence in an hour's time to give her a lunch to remember but, without a car, I was marooned. When I mentioned this to Virgilio, he told me not to worry.

'Marco and I are heading back that way now. I have to go and brief the public prosecutor, and Marco's going to the hospital to check up on Dini. We'll swing by your place, let you change into a fresh pair of trousers, and then we'll drop you off in the centre of town in good time for your lunch date. Anna can give you a lift back home again, can't she?'

'Fantastic, Virgilio. Thank you so much, but what about my van? I need to get that moved and, hopefully, repaired.'

The uniformed sergeant who had brought the news that the van was now no longer in the floodwater gave me some even better news. 'On the *commissario's* instructions, your vehicle is being taken to the police garage, where our mechanics will get it going again and clean it up, don't you worry.'

I thanked both of them most warmly but Virgilio just smiled. 'It's the least we can do. It was your idea about Cassano having faked his own strangulation that put us onto him and your idea about the wine fraud that allowed us to catch Mancini and Riccio. We owe you, Dan.'

At that moment, the lift doors behind us opened and Stokes appeared – today wearing a Def Leppard T-shirt – accompanied by none other than the old rocker himself. Digger hobbled across the lobby towards us and shook hands with all of the police officers, thanking them for resolving matters, adding his good wishes for a speedy recovery for Sergeant Dini. He spoke in English so I once again acted as interpreter. After that, he turned to me and gave me a remarkably strong handshake and a conspiratorial wink.

'Thanks, Dan. You've done me a great favour. I knew Johnny was trouble.'

'How's Florida taken it?'

The smile stayed on his face. 'Remarkably well. To be honest, I think she'd already worked out that he was a waste of space, so it's all turned out for the best.'

I remembered the promise I had made. 'Digger, did you know that Mancini threatened the old lady who's been living in the little cottage opposite the winery for the last fifty-seven years?' From the expression on his face, it was clear that this was news to him so I continued. 'She's a nice old dear, and she provided us with the evidence to convict Johnny Riccio. Would you be prepared to talk to her, to reassure her that nobody's going to evict her? I know she'd be eternally grateful.'

Digger nodded his head. 'Of course, consider it done. Stokes, get onto it.' Returning his attention to the officers, he made an offer. 'Can I give you gentlemen a little something to say thank you: a few cases of Rockstar Chianti, maybe?'

Virgilio answered for all of us. 'Thank you for the offer, but I'm afraid we can't take gifts. We were just doing our duty.' I caught Marco's eye and he winked at me. A case of the hybrid wine was definitely not what was wanted.

* * *

At exactly twelve-thirty, I walked through the door of the trattoria not far from the Arno where Anna and I had arranged to meet. We were greeted by a waiter, who led Oscar and me through the dining room and out into the beautiful courtyard. Anna was already sitting there under a parasol and she smiled and waved when she saw me. Oscar, now bone dry again, trotted over so she could make a fuss of him – and hand him down a couple of breadsticks – and I followed behind. As I bent down to kiss her, her eyes landed on the dressing on my neck.

'You look as if you've been in the wars.' Her expression became more serious. 'What's been going on?'

I sat down opposite her and stretched my legs, suddenly feeling weary but, at the same time, very happy. 'It's a long story.'

She pointed at my new polo shirt. 'Rockstar Chianti? Does this mean you've changed your mind about that stuff?'

I smiled back at her and shook my head. 'Nice polo shirt, but steer clear of the wine – at least last year's vintage. This year's may well turn out a whole lot better.' I found myself wondering who would take charge when next week's *vendemmia* started.

Hopefully, somebody with a bit more moral fibre than Fabiano Mancini. 'Now, what are we going to eat?'

There was a movement at my feet and a heavy nose landed on my knee. I looked down into Oscar's eyes. He knew and I knew what was wanted.

'Don't worry, Oscar, I haven't forgotten that steak I owe you.'

Anna looked surprised. 'Steak? What's Oscar done to deserve that?'

'To quote Virgilio, he's the best partner a detective could ever ask for.' I glanced down again. 'Thanks, buddy. You really are a good dog.'

But of course he already knew that.

* * *

MORE FROM T. A. Williams

Another book from T. A. Williams, *Murder in Verona* is available to order now here:

https://mybook.to/MurderInVeronaBackAd

ACKNOWLEDGEMENTS

Warmest thanks to Emily Ruston, my lovely editor at the marvellous Boldwood Books, as well as the rest of the Boldwood team. Sincere thanks also to Sue Smith and Emily Reader for picking up all my errors and making sure that everything makes sense. Special thanks to the talented Simon Mattacks for producing the audio versions of all the books in the Dan and Oscar series. To me, he sounds just like Dan should sound. Finally, thanks to Mariangela, my wife, whose encyclopaedic knowledge of Italian history and culture never ceases to amaze me.

ABOUT THE AUTHOR

T. A. Williams is the author of The Armstrong and Oscar Cozy Mystery Series, cosy crime stories set in his beloved Italy, featuring the adventures of DCI Armstrong and his labrador Oscar. Trevor lives in Devon with his Italian wife.

Sign up to T. A. Williams' mailing list here for news, competitions and updates on future books.

Visit T. A. Williams' website: www.tawilliamsbooks.com

Follow T. A. Williams' on social media:

x.com/TAWilliamsBooks

facebook.com/TrevorWilliamsBooks

ALSO BY T. A. WILLIAMS

The Armstrong and Oscar Cozy Mystery Series

Murder in Tuscany

Murder in Chianti

Murder in Florence

Murder in Siena

Murder at the Matterhorn

Murder at the Leaning Tower

Murder on the Italian Riviera

Murder in Portofino

Murder in Verona

Murder in the Tuscan Hills

Poison
& Pens

POISON & PENS IS THE HOME OF
COZY MYSTERIES SO POUR YOURSELF
A CUP OF TEA & GET SLEUTHING!

DISCOVER PAGE-TURNING NOVELS FROM
YOUR FAVOURITE AUTHORS &
MEET NEW FRIENDS

JOIN OUR
FACEBOOK GROUP

BIT.LYPOISONANDPENSFB

SIGN UP TO OUR
NEWSLETTER

BIT.LY/POISONANDPENSNEWS

Boldw😊d

Boldwood Books is an award-winning fiction publishing company seeking out the best stories from around the world.

Find out more at www.boldwoodbooks.com

Join our reader community for brilliant books, competitions and offers!

Follow us
@BoldwoodBooks
@TheBoldBookClub

Sign up to our weekly deals newsletter

https://bit.ly/BoldwoodBNewsletter

Printed in Great Britain
by Amazon